MW01222161

Renee Battle
Thank you!

Enjoy

Perfect Poly

A CHRONICLE OF SEXUAL ENTANGLEMENTS

RENEE BATTLE

ISBN: 978-1-7165-1424-1 (sc)
ISBN: 978-1-7165-1423-4 (e)

Library of Congress Control Number: 2020920175

Lulu Publishing Services rev. date: 10/23/2020

CONTENTS

CHAPTER 1

Summer

At 6:30 a.m., the alarm buzzed loudly throughout the room. I hit the snooze button and laid back in the bed for an extra ten minutes. I looked over at Mason as he slept peacefully. The sunlight kissed his beautiful milk chocolate skin. As I sat on the edge of the bed, I replayed last night's shenanigans in my head repeatedly. Angela smelled so amazing! She was wearing her YSL perfume that still lingered in the air. Her black plum scent filled the room.

Watching Mason and Angela was such a beautiful sight. I loved seeing them interact and embrace each other's minds and bodies. Mason really took his time with both of us last night — the kissing, the touching, the rubbing, and all the stroking made my body so aroused all over again. The alarm abruptly interrupted my thoughts, so I headed toward the bathroom to get ready for work.

As I stood in the mirror, I admired my flawless, mahogany brown skin color and how my breasts and nipples sat. They are so soft and perky. I pulled my thick, long, and curly hair back into a sleek ponytail as I smiled, all while the thoughts of all the pleasure I received filled my head. I then stepped into the shower, turned the water on at a lukewarm temperature, and let it flourish all over my body.

As the water started to roll off of me, I lathered up my sponge with cucumber scented soap and started washing my frame from head to toe. I closed my eyes and started fantasizing about the different sexual experiences that played in my mind. I always enjoyed my morning showers, which are usually the moments where I find my peace and explore my most intimate thoughts.

With my eyes still closed and mind wandering, I fantasized about how Mason stroked Angela from the back. His big mandingo went in and out of her fat pussy, throbbing and thrusting her gently. He slowly stroked her, and her juices were wetting his dick all up. Angela gripped the sheets tightly and moaned in a sexy tone. Her soft body curled up and then relaxed with every movement and stroke.

I can feel my pussy getting all wet as the memories flood my mind. So, I reached for the showerhead, turned the vow to a high speed, and opened my pussy lips as the water pressure vibrated on my clit. Just when I was about to climax, Mason knocked on the door and entered the bathroom. He opened the shower curtain, entered the shower stall, and dropped straight to his knees. He pushed me against the wall and started licking, sucking, and twirling his tongue all on my pussy lips and clit.

My legs locked up, and my eyes began to roll in the back of my head as I screamed out, "I'm cumming! I'm cumming!"

As Mason continued to bless me with his tongue, I began cumming uncontrollably and couldn't stop. As the orgasm became more intense, my legs started shaking, and I squirted all in his mouth. My pussy was throbbing as he inserted his fingers inside of me. He began to rub my g-spot, and my body trembled. Mason then stood up and planted a big messy, juicy kiss on my lips. We both smirked at each other as I tasted my own sweet juices off his lips.

After my shower, I was sitting on the bed, wondering what to wear.

"Summer! Summer!" Mason called out. "What are you over there daydreaming about?" Hello, you can't hear me calling you?" Mason shouted out.

"Yes, Mason," I answered. "Sorry I was stuck in la-la land; I'm just trying to figure out which pantsuit I want to wear today," I replied.

"Well, your text messages keep going off, and it's probably one of your other boyfriends," he said jokingly. We both chuckled.

I decided to wear my light pink Chanel suit and my red, red bottom stilettos. My red MAC lipstick that covered my succulent, chocolate lips, and my pink and red Chanel handbag went perfectly with my outfit. I pulled my hair back in a neat ponytail so that my diamond-studded earrings would show. I loved dressing nicely and maintaining my appearance.

During the day, I worked as a health inspector a couple of days and as a flight attendant on the others. I also kept myself busy as a bartender at Mason's nightclub, the Shades Lounge. I enjoyed the atmosphere and extra money, even though I only work there on Wednesday evenings. I enjoyed my work life and nightlife the same. I love living in my condominium downtown Philadelphia. It's a beautiful place located in the heart of the city.

* * *

After I got dressed and began to head out, I kissed Mason and quickly made my way to the garage. My goal was to meet my boss on time — by nine o'clock.

Beep, beep!

I hit the alarm to my black Nissan Maxima. My car was so sexy. It had all black leather seats, a sunroof, decent backup camera, GPS system, and stunning chrome rims. I synced my phone to the Bluetooth and started reading all of my text messages.

Bestie Jamal: *Good morning Summer...call me.*

My sister Autumn: *GM sis, don't forget that we work tonight. Pls call me when you are free to talk. By the way, fine ass Matteo is the pilot today.*

Clark: *Gm beautiful.*

Angela: *Good morning, baby...rise and grind. Thanks for the awesome night xoxo.*

Boss Mike: *Good morning, Summer. Please meet me at Joe's Diner on Broad and South St.*

I stopped at the local coffee shop down the street from my place and grabbed a bagel and small caramel latte, which is my favorite go-to breakfast meal for my hectic mornings.

While heading to Joe's Diner, I listened to some meditation music for ten minutes or so to clear my head. I needed that mental reset before I started my busy day. Shortly after, I hit everyone back that reached out to me, starting with Jamal.

"Summer!" he yelled through the phone, "Let me tell you about Kiesha and Jane's argument last night. It was about who can suck my dick the best!"

"So, what did you say?" I said while laughing.

"I told them let's have a dick sucking contest, and I'll judge who is the best. So, for the next couple of hours, they both went in on my dick!" Jamal voiced excitedly.

"So, who won, Jamal?" I asked anxiously.

"Shit, Kiesha...that bitch licked the plane underneath my balls. I went out and bought the girls a double-sided penis last night. They fucked the shit out of each other, and I made a video. I'll send it to you shortly," he stated.

"Okay, Jamal, I'll hit you back after work," I replied and ended our conversation. I could imagine the look on his face as he was replaying his experience from last night. I have some freaky friends, and I LOVE IT!

I pulled up to the diner, and Mike was waiting for me in the parking lot. I was still cheesing from Jamal's story. Mike just smiled and started talking because he knew not to ask me why I was smiling so hard. We then briefly discussed the plan for today.

My job was to be a regular customer and check out the environment and food service. Once I was done, I would reveal myself to be escorted to the kitchen area and complete my inspections. The look on the managers' faces is always priceless once they realize who I am.

* * *

After a long day of analyzing, I was finally finished. The diner only received a few minor citations that they were instructed to revise in two weeks. Three days out of the week, my manager and I would meet up at different restaurants, diners, mom and pop shops, supermarkets, bars, lounges, or just about any place of business that sold food.

I FaceTimed Clark as I was heading back to the office to finish my report.

"Hey, beautiful, I was just calling to see if you are free Sunday night. Maybe we can hit up a neighborhood bar and then slide to the Caribbean deck to go dancing," he suggested.

"Alright, that sounds cool to me! I'll see you Sunday. I'm working tonight and will be flying out, so I'll definitely hit you later this week. Kisses!" I replied.

After he hung up, I called my sister, Autumn.

"Hey sis, can we meet up at the convenience store near the airport around seven p.m., and then catch the shuttle over to work?" she asked.

We both agreed on this idea like we usually do. When it comes to work and money, Autumn and I are always on the same page. Our sisterly bond was so tight, and our trust was everything.

After all the running around that I've done — shopping, hair and nail appointments, and other small errands — it's finally time to take a nice shower and head to the airport to work. Tonight, will be a special one because my brother Rudolph will be doing security at this popping club in Atlanta. Some of our homegirls from Philly will be in the building celebrating my friend, Jasmine's birthday. Our brother has a security business, and he travels to different places all over the US. His guys are known to work with some famous R&B singers, rappers, ballers, and much more.

* * *

"Hey, Summer! You're glowing. What's going on with you? Who's got you smiling so hard? Did Mason and you hook up with Angela last night?" Autumn asked with a smirk and laugh.

"Yes, Autumn. We watched Netflix and chilled." I laughed.

We are some fine sisters. Men would always stare at us and wonder if we were related.

After helping the passengers to their seats and going over the safety rules, it was time to take off. All of a sudden, a pleasant cologne scent smacked me in my face.

"Damn, someone smells so good," I voiced softly to myself.

A fine gentleman lifted his head, glanced at me, and asked, "How are you, young lady?"

"Hello, Mr..."

"They call me Mr. Biggam, and the cologne you smell is called Gucci Guilty. Ms...?"

"Summer...Summer is my name, and how may I help you?"

"Can you please bring me something to drink?" he asked so politely.

"Yes, what would you like?" I said with the most flirt full smile I could give.

"Some whiskey and ginger ale."

"Sure! That will be $15."

He handed me his black card and $100 bill, and as he smirked, he said, "That's is your tip...with a small message inside."

"Okay," I said as I smiled, and he winked at me. For some reason, that made my clit jump.

* * *

After we landed and the plane was clear, I told Autumn what happened, and then I read the message.

Please call me. You won't be disappointed!

"Are you talking about the gentleman who was sitting in first class?" Autumn asked.

"Yes, he smelled so amazing!" I said.

"Yes, sis! He was fine, dark, tall, and handsome, too," Autumn agreed.

"He looks way older than us, Autumn," I replied.

"Well, I guess you just met your new sugar daddy," Autumn joked as we both laugh.

* * *

Once Autumn and I settled in Atlanta, we hit up a five-star restaurant and bar for some great quality food. You know, I can't have it any other way, being an inspector and all. We then headed to Glam Shop to get our face beat, and our hair slayed. While we were there, we saw a few reality stars. The ladies were down to earth, and the vibe was right.

Autumn and I then headed to an afternoon day party, we saw one of my favorite rapper and his fiancée, and it was so exciting. It was an all-white party, and this event was lit. The crowd was flowing, and people were partying as if it were late at night. All I could think in my head was *issa vibe!* After enjoying the day event and having a few drinks, we decided to head back to the Airbnb to freshen up and get dressed for Jasmine's party.

Hours later, Autumn and I arrived at the nightclub for the birthday party. We saw our brother doing his security thang for the event and were so happy to see him. Once inside, we headed straight to the VIP section. All eyes were on us as my sister, and I walked through the club, smelling and looking good. We noticed our friends Jasmine and China looking sexy and laced in Milano attire from head to toe. It was bananas in the club — celebrities were everywhere. They were either posted up or mingling. Money was flowing left and right, and we didn't have to pay for anything. The hospitality and love that my girls and I received from Atlanta was on a 100.

CHAPTER 2

Back to Reality

It's going to be a long week at work, and I have a lot of work to catch up on. This week I have to go to Chef's restaurant to set a date for his yearly inspection. I have a few other restaurants downtown I have to select dates for as well.

I hit up my girl Paris and told her to meet me at a new Jamaican restaurant for lunch. I called a taxi to avoid the hassle of parking. During the ride, I received a video from Mason. It was the threesome of him, Angela, and me. I started getting really horny in the back of the cab, so I pulled out my small bullet from my MCM bag. After I asked the cab driver to turn the music up, I leaned my back against the door, put one leg up, and slid my panties to the side. I had the phone in one hand and the vibrator on my clitoris. In our video, Angela was so wet, and his dick was creamed up. Mason pounded her from the back, and I took his dick out her pussy and started sucking it.

"*Ohh shitt, baby! Fuckkkkk!*" the video played.

I spit on his dick, and he stuck it back in her. He continued to moan and groan in pleasure. Angela's fat ass was bouncing on Mason, and I sucked on her soft, big titties as he continued to fuck her. This video made me wish the ride were longer because I enjoyed making myself cream in the back of the cab. I started getting stiff, my eyes rolled, and I came all over that back seat. Once I got myself together, I asked the cab driver for some paper towels. He handed it to me and winked his eye with a slight smirk.

When I finally arrived at my destination, the cab driver didn't bother to collect the fare — he must've enjoyed the ride as much as I did.

Paris was running a couple of minutes behind. Once she arrived, I told her what I just did. She laughed and told me I was so crazy.

Meanwhile, Mason sent me an old video of Angela, him, and me, and I got really horny.

After we were seated, I told Paris all about my trip to Atlanta

"Well…Paris, what's new with you, girl?" I asked.

"Girl, do you remember the brothers I told you about?" Paris asked.

"Yes, chile, what happened?"

I met two of the brothers at Shades and the other brother on Facebook. One of the brothers had a crazy foot fetish and became my sub. He loved for me to tie him up and make him follow my every command. She went into more detail about her sub, explaining how he ate food off of her feet, and she gave him a foot job, and he nutted all over her feet.

I had to ask, "What do you mean a foot job, Paris?"

"Exactly what it sounds like," Paris explained. "After making him do all kinds of demands, I used my feet oiled them up, placed them together sole to sole, held them in place tightly, and he stuck his rock, hard dick in between the small gap and start slow stroking as I glided my feet back and forth on his shaft. Paris arousing said, "That shit felt so good!"

"Wow, that's different," I stated.

Paris continued to tell me how, after many sessions, she got so horny that she demanded him to fuck her. "Girl, that nigga flipped my big ass over," she said.

Paris was the big girl of the crew and had no problem railing those niggas in. If there were ever a person to be a man-eater, it'd definitely be her.

"So, Paris, what's up with the other brothers?"

She told me another brother been hitting me up on the low and how that he was sexy asf, and of course, she eventually popped. Paris kept saying how they both had some good dick. One was sensual and great in the bed, and the other was just good for back shots. She kept saying how she'd love to have them both at one time. At that point, I knew I was in for another juicy story, so I sat back and enjoyed all the tea. Paris revealed there was another brother that she didn't know was related to them until last Friday she went to see him, and they were all there.

"All three of them were there!" Paris exclaimed. She went on telling me how wet her pussy had gotten just from the likes of them.

"What you mean all three…so what happened next? OMG…how did you pull that off?" I gasped!

"After some small talk and drinks, I told them I was about that life and asked them where they ready to gang bang me?" she revealed.

The next thing you know, Paris had her first gang bang with all three brothers. She said she told them to drop their pants and briefs. She then had them lined up in a row one by one she got them rock hard.

Shit, my pussy was beginning to get moist, listening to her tell her story. I began to grind slowly in my seat as she continued. The story went on…Paris said it was weird, but she went with the flow. She sucked on one, and the other was hitting it from the back while she was jacking the other brother off, waiting for his turn to run up in that tight wet pussy or that wet ass mouth. The rotation went on until each one bust a nice, warm load making a masterpiece all over Paris' voluptuous body.

I was so turned on that all I could do is think of what session I'd be having next. Paris' stories always get me hot and bothered, like me being constantly horny wasn't enough?

"Paris, remember I told you about the girl name Shonda who used to mess with Mason. He dated her for a little while before I was introduced to her. We hit it off fast she was a dope chic — pretty light brown skin, tall, thick thighs, and pretty brown eyes. She was super sweet and worked as a real estate agent. After a couple months of dating her heavy she had a family emergency and stop talking to us. I want to reach out to her again, but she didn't reply to my last text, so what do you think?"

"Summer, that sound like a crazy relationship. Let's just call it entanglement."

After we enjoyed our lunch, I contacted Chef to see what time he wanted to meet. He stated he wanted me to meet him after work and stay the night with him.

* * *

I love waking up to the smell of breakfast in bed. It was truly one of my favorite things.

I stayed with Chef last night at his place in New Jersey.

"Breakfast in bed, baby," he announced as he kissed me. "I made you your favorite —salmon cakes, shrimp and cheese grits, and a Belgium waffle with strawberry and bananas."

Chef is so fine, and he reminds me of a light pecan skin toned Michael B. Jordan. He had smooth tan skin and a smile to die for.

"This breakfast tastes so good," I stated.

"Not as good as you," he replied.

Damn, my pussy started to get moist as I listened to his voice.

"Are you going to eat with me, babe?" I asked.

"No, once you're done, I'm going to eat you and give you a nice full body massage."

Chef's strong hands drenched in massage oil felt so good on my back. He took his time and rubbed all over my body from head to toe. Once he reached my ass, the massage was over. He lifted me up, asked me to get in a doggy style position, and licked and sucked me from the back. He gently flipped me on my back and started massaging my clit with his tongue. His mouth felt so good as he stroked his tongue in and out, and my pussy gripped his tongue.

I started squirting all over his bed, and the sheets were soaked. He locked his mouth on my clit, and I had one of the best orgasms ever. The pleasure had me stuck, and I couldn't move my legs. Eventually, they started shaking because he continued to stroke my g-spot until I began to squirt again. He caught my juices in his mouth and then spat it back on my pussy while looking up at me and caressing my thick thighs. That got me wetter! Chef made sure I was always treated like a queen, and he always catered to me.

He whispered in my ear, "Your pussy is dripping wet and tastes so good."

"Oh, Chef..." I loudly moaned as he lifted up my legs, held them high in the air, and slid his manhood in my tight wet pussy.

He stroked slowly in and out, back and forth, and in and out again. He began to speed up, and he started pounding my pussy. He pounded me so good until I gushed all over him. He then began to suck on my titties as he stroked slower and slower. My pussy tightened up around his thick eight-inch penis until we both climaxed together. I lowered my head onto his chest and let out a sigh of release. He always knows how to take me to ecstasy.

I fell asleep and woke up three hours later, still feeling tired after the long week. Chef was still knocked out also.

CHAPTER 3

Shades Lounge

It's Wednesday night, and Shades is going to be lit for Wagon Wednesday and karaoke night. I got fresh to death as always and headed to the club.

Mason was looking so fucking good in his designer shirt, Rolex watch, and Gucci shoes. The club is located in the north side of the city, which is pretty close to downtown. Tonight, I will be giving away Henny shots to all the ladies that twerk the best. I'm super psyched about all that ass that's gonna be bouncing around. The DJ's got club jumping, the neighborhood ballers are in the building, and the ladies are looking super sexy.

Black yelled out, "It's time to make it rain!"

His homie Jason shouted, "Summer, pour up 50 shots!" It was about to be a VIBE!

Black and Jason were the main players of the neighborhood and made sure any party or event they attended stayed lit. With my help and sex appeal, parties always start and end well. I'm a part of an adult social club, and I'm well known in the city, which allows me to have a huge following. The adult club is a diverse group of mature people ranging from ages 21 and up, and we all love to party and socialize. People travel all over the tri-state to come see me in action.

For tonight's event, I'm wearing a see-through belly top and a black bra, tight booty shorts that look painted on me, and some Gucci sandals. I watched Mason from across the room, and he looks so good tonight. Seeing him work and handle his business always turns me on. He is a boss, is well respected, and the ladies love him. The best part about Mason and me is that we bag females together. We move alike in so many different ways.

the DJ screamed over the microphone, "Who's up next to sing karaoke?"

This thick redbone with dreads and a fat ass gets on the microphone and sings the shit out of an old school Monica song, and she was eying me down from across the room throughout her performance. Her sex appeal was amazing. After she finished, it was time to turn up.

I told the DJ to play some Megan Thee Stallion or City Girls to get all the girls in the mood to shake their ass and get loose. As the drinks flowed and the crowd got hype, I told the chic with the dreads to come twerk for me. I caressed her thighs as she started grinding on me. The fellas were going crazy and throwing money in the air as they enjoyed the view.

My boo, Bossy, stepped in the building looking all fly as usual. She had the crew with her: Dre, Amber, Terry, Jane, Keith, Tim, Aaron, Kiesha, and Eric.

I poured several shots of Henny and Jose Cuervo as people continued to buy the bar out. Da Baby and Lil Baby played in the background as people continued to mingle, drink, dance, and enjoy the vibe. The club was packed, and security was tight as the night went on.

"Alright, everyone, it's two a.m. You don't have to go home, but you have to get out of here!" I yelled on the microphone as we wrapped up the night.

After gathering all my tips and cashing out, I was ready to go. Once we were closed completely, I noticed the red bone, thick chic with the fat ass waiting out front. I asked her if she was okay, and she said she would be much better if she can go with me. I told her I was with my male partner, and it seemed as if she had no problem with that. She said that it was all good and introduced herself as Secret. I introduced myself and Mason to her as well, and after mingling for a few minutes, we hopped in the whip and headed to my condominium.

* * *

After Secret and I arrived at my place, we talked and waited for Mason to grab a blunt and some loud. I offered Secret a drink, and she requested wine. Once Mason arrived home, I turned on some old school hip-hop R&B in my bedroom. Secret asked can she do a dance on the pole for us. I didn't turn down that offer. She was so sexy, and I knew that Mason and I would enjoy seeing her dance and move her hips. Chris Brown and Usher's song played softly in the background.

♪♪*Fuck you back to sleep, girl, rock you back...*♪♪

Secret danced on the pole so seductive. She wore black eyeliner around her eyes that made her look even more appealing. She started twirling while holding onto the pole and began going up and down poppin' her ass sensually. Mason and I got off the bed and started making it rain, throwing money all over her ass. She got up off the ground, looked me in my eyes, and then began to suck on my titties.

Mason joined the fun and started sucking the other one. They shared my body and felt so good...I felt like I was in heaven. We made our way to the bed, and I told her to lay on top of me and open her legs. Mason laid on the bed and started eating out our pussy, one at a time. He gently fingered one and ate the other, and then he would switch. We switched positions, and Secret sat on his face while I rode his dick. Secret and I kissed and rubbed on each other, enjoying each other's curves and body. While she was face fucking him, I saw Secret's juices running down his cheeks. She moaned so loud and locked her legs around his face to where he couldn't breathe. I got off his dick and started kissing him, and I tasted her. Secret tasted so sweet.

For the rest of the night, we continued to fuck, lick, and suck on each other. Mason enjoyed the double head. I licked his balls while she sucked him. We French kissed all over his dick. He started to cum, and I swallowed all nine and a half inches of his dick down my throat. He embraced every second until he began to get weak and started bitching. We took an hour break, showered together, and washed each other up.

Our chemistry was heavy (panting), kissing and rubbing each other.

"Come on, ladies, let's make a movie tonight," Mason suggested. Secret said she was with it.

Back in the bedroom, Mason set the camera up on the tripod.

Secret put Cardi B and Megan The stallion new song on "WAP" (WET ASS PUSSY). The beat dropped, and I joined her on the pole, and we put a quick show on for Mason.

We rapped the song lyrics to him, "YEAH, YEAH, YEAH!"

I crawled on top of Mason and whispered in his ear, "Spit in my mouth and look in my eyes."

Secret Started saying, "Yeah, you fucking with some wet ass pussy."

I yelled, "Come on, Secret. Hop on his dick and spell my name!" She rode his dick while I spat in his mouth and kissed him.

"I'ma cum all over your dick, and I'ma suck it off," Secret voiced.

I laid on my back while Secret buried her face in my pussy, and I gripped her head tightly while I called out Mason's name, moaning softly. "How do her pussy feel?"

He responded, "Baby, she feels so good."

As the sensation continued to build up, I grabbed Secret's dreads so tight she was unable to catch her breath, and I exploded all over her face screaming, "Oh, Mason! Ohhhhh, Mason! Yessss, baby, I'm cumming!"

We locked eyes, and to my surprise, Mason yelled, "Summmmmerrr, I'm about to bust!"

Oh, shit! Mason held his big dick trying to control his nut and told Secret to turn around and catch his nut, then he cream pied all over her face.

The video was cut short but straight to the point.

CHAPTER 4

BDSM

(Bondage/Discipline, Dominance/ Submission, and Sadism/Masochism)

My work week went by past pretty fast, and Friday night was fast approaching. Tonight, Autumn and I planned to go to Mason's bar, Shades, for drinks, food, and hookah. After Shades, we arranged to stop by Jamal's private after hour called, Pendulum. It's a BDSM experience and environment. Sir Charles will be doing private sessions with hot wax, whips, bondage, and blindfolds. I loved his variety of toys and big or small vibrators.

Club Pendulum is a swinger's, members-only club. People travel from across the USA to attend this private club most of the time. The after-hour spot has many rooms. There's a bull ride in the middle of the black glow room, the red room is equipped with whips and chains, the blue room is for weed smokers, and there is also a bar that's set up with swings and comfortable lounge chairs. The white room is where the dance floor, second bar area, and the DJ set up is located. There are five private and spacious rooms with beds that are designated as the play areas. The bathroom and cleaning stations are also in each area to ensure everyone is following the protocols. You gotta keep that couth and peen clean. After 3:30 a.m., everyone has to dress down in nudity or sexy lingerie. If not, exit stage left.

The Session

Sir Charles and I go way back. He's a really cool, laid back man. He has such a nice sex appeal. He is tall, brown skin, and built like the famous actor Lance Gross. Sir Charles also has a really strong presence about him but maintains a gentle touch.

"Hey, Summer," he greeted with his deep voice.

Whenever Sir Charles speaks to me, I get goosebumps...it's almost as if his voice sends chills down my spine. We greeted each other with a hug, and he gives me soft kisses on each cheek.

"It's been a long week. I want the special. My body needs it!" I explained.

As he put the blindfold on my eyes, I sat anxiously in the chair with him standing behind me. He tied my hands to the chair and told me to relax and to be comfortable. I relaxed my body as best as I could and cleared my mind. Sir Charles started with the Adrenaline Pinwheel, rolling it up and down my back and arms. *There go those goosebumps.* I let out my first of many sighs. Then he gently poured hot oil on my back and started massaging me. He was hitting all the tight areas. If there were any thoughts in my head, they were all gone for sure.

Once he was finished with the sensual hot oil, he poured multi-colored hot wax on me, one color at a time. The heat of the hot wax and the essence of the hot oils was the exact mixture I needed to take me to a euphoric state. I could see the artwork he was making as the hot wax began to harden in its place from the mirrors that he had strategically had in place for his subjects to witness his masterpieces. Sir Charles then got his daggers out. He used three different ones before he found the right one; the exact one that my body the reaction he was looking for. The metal blade grazed up and down my back and arms, putting me at ease. Soft music played in the background, so I closed my eyes and enjoyed the moment.

"Okay, Summer, are you ready?" Sir Charles quizzed in a deep, soft voice. He asked me to stand up. "It's time to tie you to the X-Cross."

I enjoyed being restrained. I was in the spread eagle position facing the cross — my wrists and ankles where buckle down. I asked for him to keep the blindfold on me to enjoy every sensation. When I have my sessions with Sir Charles, I become more submissive. I love his sensual touches. He used the flogger and paddle on my juicy round booty.

"Yesssss, Sir Charles!" I moaned. We are finished, and now it's time for the finale.

He turned my favorite vibrator on. The sound of it got the juices flowing, so there was no need for and lubricant he turned it up to the highest level, and he placed it on my pussy. I felt myself starting to orgasm because of the intensity. I let out another sigh, and I screamed with the softest, pleasant moan. It made Sir Charles' dick hard. That was the first time I ever notice that happen to him. He began to blush, and just then, my vagina started pouring like a rain forest. I had multiple orgasms from the entire experience with Sir Charles, and I so deserved all that pleasure I received that night.

CHAPTER 5

Mr. Clark

Sunday had approached, and I slept in all day — no work, just some me time. Once I woke up, it was around two p.m., and I realized that I missed a call from Clark.

Clark: *Good morning, beautiful. I hope you're ready for me tonight. Meet me at my place around 9 p.m.*

I read the text message with a smile, thinking about what he meant exactly.

Shortly after, I continued my day with meditation and breathing exercises. I felt so relieved afterwards and had the appetite for a delicious green smoothie. After my smoothie, I felt more energized so, I decided to run on the treadmill for about 45 minutes. I watched my favorite television series while I was on there. I then wrapped up my Sunday household duties. My clothes were washed, and the condo was thoroughly cleaned, so I should be good for the remainder of the week.

As I was getting dressed, I thought about what would fit the mood for tonight. Clark always gets excited when I look extra sexy, so I decided to wear heels and something tight that snugs my curves.

I decided to wear a sexy red dress that I recently bought from one of my favorite high-end stores. I'll wear my beautiful hair down my back, in curls. He loves that. My designer wedges will be perfect for the night because it matches my dress, and it fits the occasion. We are going to a Caribbean deck. The wedges will allow me to dance all night. My nails, feet, and lashes were done yesterday — so tonight I'll be looking stunning from head to toe. The Chanel Chance perfume tops everything. It smells so amazing. Clark loves when I smell good...he always recognizes every little detail about me.

* * *

I arrived at Clark's place at nine o'clock on the dot. I made sure that I was on time because he always teases me about my lateness. I noticed that he always gives me an earlier time so that I'll arrive on schedule. We decided to first stop past a neighborhood bar for a few drinks and food.

Clark stood at 6'2, had dark chocolate skin, and curly hair with a masculine and athletic build. He wore glasses and looked charming all the time. Clark was very handsome and dressed really conservative. It was something special about him, and he drove me wild. We dated years ago, prior to my seeing Mason. Clark and I had an incredibly unique bond. Maybe it was our conversation or his charm that turned me on. I was so comfortable with him. He would be so silly, crack jokes, and even randomly dancing around when we would be chilling and listening to music. He would clear the floor in his living room so we could slow dance and hold each other. He was a hopeless romantic.

The club's music was so loud that we could hear it up the block as we drove toward the direction of the event. The line was exceptionally long, so it's a good thing we didn't have to wait. My brother's partner was head of security that night, so we slid right in. As soon as Clark and I entered, we headed straight to the bar to order drinks. We were ready to get the night flowing. I ordered vodka, and Clark chose Henny. My song started playing in the background "Drogba (Joanna)" by Afro B

♫♫Joanna, your busy body
Busy tonight

Joanna
Make you no dey dull me tonight
Joanna, your busy body giving me life, oh
Hey, life, eh...♪♪

I started winding and grinding my ass on Clark, and he loved all that shit. He grabbed my waist closed to his and started moving at my pace. Eventually, he pulled his phone out and started recording me. I made sure I was extra sexy and seductive for him, and he started lifting my red dress a little. Clark got behind me, grabbed my waist, and I rub my ass so hard on his dick.

The energy at Caribbean Deck was lit, and the Soca music was blasting. I was twirling my Trinidad bandana in the air, shaking my ass to the beat, bouncing and jumping up and down. The night was sensual, and Clark made me feel like the only woman in the building. He is a very dominant man, the perfect gentleman but definitely a bully in the bedroom. Grinding against him had my mind thinking about all the mind-blowing sex we have. As I danced on him all night, I couldn't help but think about the way he stroke my pussy until I have multiple orgasms. Right here, right now, he is mind fucking me on the dance floor.

CHAPTER 6

Jamal's Cookout

All the tents and tables are set up, and Kiesha and Jane were up all-night cooking. This is our annual lifestyle pool party/ cookout. For this event, I have people coming from all over, so we about to be lit.

I hired someone to cook all the grilled food. Now it's time to chill, then get dressed before the party. While relaxing on the couch, Kiesha walks pass with a pair of thongs on and a cropped top. I reach and smacked her on the ass.

"Damn Jamal, you about to start some shit." We both laughed.

"Come give me some head while I watch this game. Damn, Kiesha your mouth feel so wet." After about fifteen minutes, I busted all in her mouth. "Good girl, baby."

* * *

Finally, the time has come for the guest to arrive, and my homeboy brought about ten ladies with him. I noticed this one female who stood out to me. She stood about five feet even, very petite little booty and small breasts, chocolate, and ratchet. I pictured doing something's wild to her in my head. I introduced myself, and she had a big smile on her face showing all her pretty white teeth.

"My name is Ashley."

"I am Jamal. This is my home. I share it with myself and two wives."
The look on her face showed curiosity

"Okay, I hear that. Tell me more. I would love to meet them."

I gave Ashley a tour of my home and introduced her to my ladies. Jane gave her a nice welcoming hug. "Nice to meet you, Ashley."

Kiesha was in the kitchen and gave her a friendly greeting.

"Nice to meet you all. Your home is beautiful," Ashley stated. "Can I help you with anything in the kitchen?

"I'm okay, Ashley. Enjoy the party. We will catch up with you later."

Finally, the guest has arrived, so the house and pool were at capacity. Women are looking good half-naked. The movie is being filmed. It's a twerk fest ass, ass, ass, ass, shaking everywhere with money being thrown in the air. The fellas have the drinks on deck.

"Everyone has to get naked after 1 a.m.," the DJ announced
Everyone screamed, "Hell, yeah!"

The party was flowing. Ashley sneaks up behind and grabs my hands and pulls me toward the tree in between the cars in the back right corner where no one is located.

"So, Jamal, are you allowed to play without your ladies?"

"Yes," Jamal answered.

She pushed me up against the tree and kissed me. I was shocked but with the shit. I picked her little ass up and placed her on the hood of someone Royal blue Charger. I pulled the condom out my pocket so fast I'm not even sure if it was on right. This little bitch was not ready for all this pipe. I had her in the stand and deliver position and pounded the shit out her tiny ass. Ashley's pussy felt tight and gripped my dick tighter and tighter until I felted a warm sensation on my penis. This shit felt amazing

"I can't wait for us to have some fun with the ladies," I told Ashley.

"Yes, daddy fuck me harder! I'm about to cum again.

"Shit, I'm cumming too, DAMNNN!"

Ashley hopped off the hood of the car and pulled her skirt down and said, "I'll be ready to play with the ladies later," and walked away.

I went to the house and cleaned myself up thinking in my head how I'm about to explain this entanglement to the ladies when I looked up, and Jane was in the room changing her clothes. I told her what just took place, and that Ashley appeared as if she was interested in playing with us tonight.

Jane smiled. "Had asked if I had cleaned off yet?"

"I'm about to."

Jane walked over to me and started tongue kissing me. "Lay on the bed and open up your legs up," I ordered.

I laid flat on my stomach and started eating Jane's pussy like fresh watermelon on a warm summer day. I placed my tongue on her clitoris just how she likes and wrote the ABC's with my tongue. Once I made it to O and circled back and forth a few times and made a slurping noise, Jane tightened her legs up, grabbed my ear, and all fluid flowed in my mouth like a gusher. My chin had a long, slimy cum string hanging to my chest.

"Jamal, now. I'm ready for more."

"Later, baby," I responded as I cleaned up and headed back to the party.

My homie Eric had a money machine that was spraying bills everywhere. All I see is the ladies stuffing their bra, panties, purses, or whatever they can grab to scoop the money up. Eric's a manager of an up-and-coming rapper from Philly, and he will perform his latest hit. "Chicks Going Wild".

"Yo, E!"

"Yo, bro!" and we greeted each other with a handshake. "I want you to meet my artist Big Kev."

"Welcome."

"Thanks for having me tonight and allowing me to perform my single. We plan to shoot a scene for my music video tonight. Is that okay with you, Jamal?"

"Yes, it's perfect."

"Summer, Ayooo, Summer. Come here. It's someone I want you to meet."

Big Kev hit me on my armed and asked, "Who is that bro? Is that you?"

"No, that's my best friend. My ladies are standing over there near the bar.

"Ladies?"

"Yup, Kiesha and Jane. We are in a poly relationship."

"Damn! That's fire."

"Hello, gentlemen," Summer greeted.

"You know Eric, and this is Big Kev," I introduced.

"Hello, nice to finally meet you. Eric has told me good things about you," Summer stated.

"Nice to meet you, beautiful," Big Kev flirted.

Summer blushed.

"If you're not busy this weekend, I would love to have you be a part of my music video as a leading lady," Big Kev suggested.

"Sure, hit me up on social media. We will rap," Summer agreed.

"Say less," Big Kev stated.

Summer walked away to meet Angela at the driveway.

"Shorty is nice, Jamal," Big Kev commented.

"Hit her up she dope as fuck," I encouraged.

"The party definitely is a VIBE!"

* * *

This party is epic, and it's going down in history as one of my biggest cookouts. The evening continued to flow, and the party didn't end until five a.m. Jane and Ashley were in the pool all morning. Kiesha was cleaning up, and some people were utilizing the bedrooms for their own private fun. All I can smell when I walked into my house was weed, liquor, and sex.

The Music Video

Big Kev had set up a private lunch for both of us. We talked for a while, and he a very humble guy. His personality is dope and considering the type of money he has he's down to earth. He explained he's in the streets, but he's investing in his music career, and he has his own label. He likes to travel and that he would like to take me away to an island somewhere I can pick, and he will pay.

He took me to the mall to buy me a few outfits for the photoshoot and music video later. I told him I wanted my girlfriend Secret to be a part of it because she a known dancer in Philadelphia and can help promote and get him even more followers. I purchased her a couple of cute sexy tight outfits as well.

* * *

Later back at the studio, Secret walked me through a couple sexy poses and moves I can do during the video. During the shoot, we both were looking super sexy. Kev's song was catchy, Slow, and fast pace upbeat tempo and a booty-shaking hit.

Big Kev was all over me, and I was all over him. He stood about 6'3 husky, brown skin with curly hair. He said he was cuban and black. He smelled amazing, he dressed to impress, and he enjoyed the finer things in life.

During the shoot, he placed the palm of his hand on my ass. I was a turn on, but I couldn't show him. I had to play hard to get because he seemed like a keeper. However, I have too much going on to entertain him at the moment, but in time I will.

Big Kev's song made the radio, and it became a Philly banger for the rest of the summer.

CHAPTER 7

Mr. Biggam

A few weeks passed, and everything was going smoothly between my personal life, social life, and work life. I've been working so hard that I even received a promotion at work. Autumn and I were heading to Atlanta Monday night. I reached out to Mr. Biggam and informed him I'd be arriving around eight p.m. I filled Autumn in on some things I've learned about him after texting him over the past few weeks. He is 48 years old, owns an IT company, and travels a lot because of work. He lives alone in a nice home, his son is away at college, and his wife passed away a few years ago.

Every week since Mr. Biggam's and I met, he has been sending me roses to my job. He shows me he has a gentleman side to him. I really had intentions of enjoying his company...but it was a warm summer night in Atlanta, and all I wanted to do was chill in the hotel room, order room service and watch TV with my sister. However, Mr. Biggam had plans to take me to a restaurant. He also told me I didn't need to pack a suitcase or any extra clothes because he sent me a generous amount of money to my Cash App to go shopping.

Once we landed, Autumn and I went to Lenox Mall to make a stop at Saks Fifth Ave. I purchased an off-the-shoulder BCBG Max Azria, light gold cocktail dress, I and found some slingback heels for tonight.

First Date

Biggam arrived around 9:30 p.m., and he pulled up in a 2020 red Tesla Model 3 with tinted windows. I was overly impressed. He was a fine man for his age. He was in shape, had swag, and a nice sense of style. Most people say that he reminded them of Idris Eba when he played Stringer Bell in *The Wire*.

Our date was off to a good start. We conversed in the car as we headed to a popular steak and seafood restaurant in downtown Atlanta. The atmosphere in the restaurant was very relaxing. I ordered lobster, shrimp, scallops, mashed potatoes with butter, and sautéed asparagus. Biggam ordered a porterhouse steak, loaded mashed potatoes, and steamed broccoli. As we talked throughout the night, I told him about my lifestyle.

I shared that I'm a part of a swingers club, and he explained that one of his clients owned a private swingers club in Atlanta called The Loft. He explained that he has never been there and would love to experience it with me. He called the club owner, and he told us to come after midnight.

* * *

Biggam and I finally arrived at the club, and his friend Brett met us and gave us a tour. It was a massive 3,300 square feet building of sexy lifestyle play space with five private rooms, a group room, a dance floor equipped with stripper poles and a bar area, lounge areas, locker rooms, and a live DJ.

After taking our first round of shots together, we headed to the group room. A Caucasian lady walked up to us, and she asked me if she could taste me. She was sexy, resembling Sophia Bush — short, with big tits. She squatted down, opened my legs, and started licking every inch of my vagina. Her tongue softly glided in and out, and her lips gently massaged my clitoris. I looked over at Biggam, and he was stroking his manhood. I started to moan and felt my body quiver. My eyes started rolling, and a rush took over my body. I screamed, "I'm cummmming!"

I held her face in place, busted a big nut, and she sucked every drop up. She licked around her mouth and said, "Thank you, baby, you taste so good."

She looked at Biggam, rubbed one hand on her pussy, and took her other hand to help him stroke his cum right out his dick. She opened wide, and he busted all over her face — she was definitely a freak and didn't care that it got in her hair and eyes. After the pleasure, she complimented both of us and explained that she wasn't expecting to run into such a sexy couple. She was really approachable and outgoing, I wish we could've talked to her longer, but she rushed to the lockers to freshen up and clean herself up.

Biggam and I sat in the lounge area, staring at each other in a daze, a little shocked at what just happened. Biggam then stood up, zipped his pants up, and told me to freshen up because he had a surprise for me back at his place. I was startled and did as he said, anxious for this surprise. The night was already spontaneous, so I was ready for anything and everything. Shortly after I was finished and ready, valet pulled his car to the front of the club, and we made our way back to his place.

* * *

We arrived at a gated community, full of oversized homes. Biggam's property had a long driveway, and the landscape on his property was beautiful. Once inside, I instantly felt comfortable.

"Summer, would you like something to drink?" Biggam asked.

"No thanks, big daddy...I'm ok," I replied.

"Well, make yourself at home. I'm going to hop in the shower," he stated.

I chilled in the living room area and connected my music to his Bluetooth speaker until he was finished. His house was beautifully decorated and immaculate. We sat on his outdoor deck by the fire and talked for a few hours.

31

He told me he was born and raised in Houston, Texas, and he moved to New York for college, and that's where he met his wife. After they graduated, they moved to Washington, DC and shortly after his wife announced that she was pregnant with their son. Eventually, Biggam started his own IT Company, and they relocated to Atlanta. His wife passed away a few years ago — shortly after their son graduated high school. He didn't quite go into detail on exactly how she died, and I didn't bother to ask. I was just happy enough that he was comfortable enough to tell me about his good and dark times.

I enjoyed listening to his life stories. His tone is so deep and sexy. Aside from that, Biggam is a brilliant man. I was so wet I could feel it on my legs, and I love that he is different from what I'm used to. After he finished telling me about his background, I shared my story with him as well. I told Biggam that I'm well established, with no kids, and I was raised with both parents in Philadelphia. I shared that I have an older brother and one younger sister, eleven months younger than me. I also explained that I met my closest friends in college, and they are the ones who introduced me to the lifestyle.

"I prefer to practice polygamy," I said, a little hesitant.

Biggam's eyes grew really wide, and he seemed surprised. He said that he was familiar with that type of lifestyle and relationship dynamic. It was good to know that he wasn't completely oblivious or judgmental of my preference.

I continued to share more with Biggam and told him that I'm active in a social club where adults occasionally meet up in public places like restaurants, bars, clubs, movies, and bowling, and much more. After more small talk, he handed me a large gift bag. Inside was a designer MCM pocketbook with plane tickets inside. I smiled and looked at the tickets which read first-class Houston, TX. It appears like we were going to his home town for my birthday. We always talked about visiting there together and because I have never been. He told me that his family has a ranch there, and that he had plans to show me around.

We cuddled up, and I eventually fell asleep in his arms. After so much time connecting, conversing, and laying up, I finally woke up and realized it was nearly the morning time. Biggam brought me breakfast and took me back to the hotel. I kissed him on the forehead and cheek and told him that we definitely need to see each other more often.

CHAPTER 8

Autumn

I'm exhausted, but I have a date tonight. After departing from my sister, I texted Chad to meet me at my hotel room around nine p.m. I met Chad at the club the night of Jasmine's party. He owns seven gyms in Atlanta. He was in the VIP section next to ours that night. He was a pretty boy. He was tall, fair skin with green eyes, and a body like Nathan Owens, the famous model. He sent a $500 bottle to our section that night, and after that, he came over and introduced himself. I told him my name, and I asked him if he knew my brother, and he stated yes, he comes to the gym with a couple basketball players some time and workout.

The next morning, we had breakfast in downtown Atlanta. Tonight, I plan on hooking up with him when I come back to visit Atlanta. We talked on the phone every day since we met and even had phone sex, and we video chatted a lot.

* * *

Once I arrived at the hotel to check in. I enter my room, and it was rose petal and candles lit and balloons everywhere. Jazz music was playing in the background, and a massage table was set up. Chad was standing shirtless oiled up, looking so sexy. He looked over at me, telling me to come over to him. Once I approached him, he grabbed me and locked his lips on mine. Your lips are so soft, sexy. Now, I'm going to give you a quick wash, and then a nice full body massage.

As I laid there on the table, I closed my eyes and took a deep breath. Chad started on my shoulders, rubbing in a circular motion moving to each arm, pulling and rubbing back and forth. He moved to the center of my back onto my legs. Standing in the middle, he binds his arms straight to reach directly under my buttocks. He placed my toes in his mouth, sucking in between every toe. The sensation flowing through my body sent chills down my spine. The way Chad grab my ass, he asks me to get on all fours. I felt his wet mouth and tongue lick between my ass. Once he put his tongue in my ass, I let out a sigh.

Chad carried me to the bed. "Is it okay if I restrain you to the bed?"

"Yes, daddy!"

"What should our safe word be?"

"Red, the color red," I replied. "Or three taps to the bed when I don't like something."

"Okay, Ms. Autumn."

Chad places a blindfold over my eyes and a gag ball in my mouth.

"Okay, I'ma put some whipped cream on your stomach first."

To be honest, it tickled a bit, but I was unable to move. Then he started softly kissing me on my side and stomach area. It was plenty of foreplay, and I enjoyed every moment. Chad teased and pleased me. He reached my lips below and separated my lips and French kiss my pussy lips.

"Ohhhhhh!"

Chad is exploring my body in ways no other man has before. He was making love to my mind, body, and soul. I Imagined my husband and wife in my head and pictured all of us entangled with one another during this sexual experience. Just as I was having freaky thoughts in my head about them, I started to have an orgasm. My body shifted up, locked, and I couldn't move (literally). He kept sucking, applying pressure, and I started squirted uncontrollably. He could feel all my juices on his soft full lips.

"Autumn, the last part of our session will be the wand. It's perfect for clitoral stimulation."

After three powerful rounds of that, I tapped out being unleashed. I laid there lifeless like I just had an out-of-body experience. He started the Jacuzzi, and we chilled for the rest of the night. Until we meet again, Chad.

CHAPTER 9

Philadelphia Here I Come

Summer

On the flight back to our hometown, I told Autumn about my night with Biggam.

"Well, sis, you're not the only one who had fun. Chad planned an unforgettable night that was all about me. He's a pleaser for sure. He didn't even want to have penetration. The look on my face was priceless — *damn, Autumn.* We laughed and shared our fun Atlanta experience.

"Summer, when are we going to plan your birthday party? It's only a month away, and it needs to be the party of the year!" Autumn quizzed.

"Well, I know Mason is throwing me an all-white party at Shades on the 20th. Chef wants to cook me a private dinner, and then Clark will take me to Miami after my birthday weekend. I also made plans to go see Mr. Biggam, and he will take me to Houston within the first week of September," I explained.

* * *

Once we landed, I headed straight home. I seriously missed my condo and comfortable bed. When I opened the door, it smelled so good. The candles were lit and rose petals were on the floor leading to the bedrooms.

There were dozens of roses all over the condominium. There was a note attached.

Summer, my love, it has been a wonderful six years with you in my life. I want you to head to the master bathroom.

I was instantly shocked and disappointed that I forgot that it was our seven-year anniversary. I walked into the bathroom, and candles were lit around the tub. Mason was sitting in the tub with his eyes wide, filled with love. I removed my clothes and got in the warm bubble bath. Mason gave me the biggest and most passionate kiss on the lips. Our lips locked, and we embraced each other.

"Happy seven years, baby. I miss you so much," I said as I hugged Mason.

He asked me about my night, and I told him it was very eventful. We both laughed, and he said, "I can only imagine with your crazy ass. Tomorrow, we are catching a flight to the Bahamas for five days," Mason said. "I already talked to your boss, and I will close the bar until we return," he continued.

I was filled with excitement. Mason really knew everything that I loved and needed — I couldn't wait to get away and see the blue waters and beautiful sky.

After our bath, we entered the bedroom. I told Mason to take a seat. He pulled me close to him and started French kissing me. He rubbed all over my body. He started sucking my breasts softly and licking my nipples with his tongue. I got so aroused, but I told him to relax because I had something in store for him.

"I have a surprise for you," I said seductively.

I dried off, moisturized my skin with my favorite scented lotion, and changed into my red, two-piece lace lingerie set with bikini-cut bottoms. I put on my high stiletto shoes and patted my drenching, wet hair with my towel. I handed Mason a bottle of oil, and he rubbed my body up and down. I turned on Beyoncé's "Dance For You", and I slowly walked around the chair he was sitting in, bent down, and whispered in his ear,

"Tonight I'm going to dance for you." I wined my body to the beat and started going up the pole until I reached the top as Beyoncé's song played.

> ♫♫*I'll be rockin' on my babe rockin' rockin' on my babe*
> *Swirlin' on you babe swirlin' swirlin on you babe*
> *Baby lemme put my body on your body*
> *Promise not to tell nobody 'cause*
> *It's bout to go down...*♫♫

I dropped down the pole slowly, keeping my eyes on Mason. Once I was midway in the air, Mason stood up, walked over to me, and said, "Stay right there."

He wrapped his powerful arms around me and placed my legs over his strong shoulders. He slid my panties to the side and started eating my pussy and licking my ass. His hands were palming my ass as he was eating my pussy like it was his last meal. He used his warm mouth on my clit and sucked so hard until I creamed. Mason then picked me up, gently placed me on his shoulders, and pinned me against the wall. I grabbed his head, and he tongue-fucked me for like ten minutes, which seemed like an eternity. I came all on his face, and he threw me on the bed. His dick was rock hard. I laid on my back with my face hanging off the edge of the bed and told him to face fuck me.

I opened my mouth wide, and he slid every bit of his ten-inch penis down my throat. It filled my mouth completely, and so much saliva dripped down his legs. Mason slid me back on the bed, and we continued with the 69 position. I started squirting everywhere. We then switched up into the doggie style position. I felt every inch of his dick entering my canal. I moaned and arched my back even more so that I can feel it all.

"Summer, your pussy is so fucking wet. Damn girl, oh my god! I love you, Summer!" Mason shouted as he smacked my ass.

In mid-stroke, he stopped and started licking my pussy from the back. He entered me again and began to slowly stroke me. I started squirting again. He stopped the penetration, bent down to catch some of my juices in his mouth, and then spit it on my ass. He started fucking me so hard until my pussy gripped his dick so tight, and I could feel his dick throbbing inside of me. I gripped his dick with my pussy muscles, and he let out one of the biggest, sexy, manliness moans ever.

"Summmmmer!" he called out loudly.

Mason exploded deep in my pussy. His cum was so warm and creamy. I jumped up, put my mouth on his dick, and sucked the rest out of him. Our night ended with aggressive, passionate sex. We definitely missed each other.

* * *

The next morning, we headed to sunny Bahamas. Signs were plastered all over the airport. *Welcome to Nassau, Bahamas.*

I was so ready to get settled and enjoy the beautiful weather. Mason and I decided that we will rest for a few. The beautiful Atlantis Resort is where we will stay. We had so much planned for our trip — Aqua ventures, the water park for a day, swimming with the dolphins, Adrastea Garden Zoo, a candlelight dinner on the beach, and so much more. I knew that this trip would be everything that I could imagine.

Walking around the strip mall, the salespeople were very pushy, and it was a lil stressful because they came off rude. A nice-looking woman approached us and handed us a flyer. The flyer read of a swinger pool party.

I showed Mason, and we both laughed.

"What are the odds?" he said with a big smile on his face.

We headed to a restaurant after we order our food and drinks. I told Mason to meet me in the restroom.

Once he entered, I locked the door, pushed him against the wall, got into a squat position, unzipped his pants, and whipped his dick out. I sucked his manhood so good he could barely move. I opened my mouth, closed it tight, shoved it down my throat while gripping his ass cheeks so he couldn't move. I gagged and squirted some on the floor. I motioned my head back and forth, making his dick nice and juicy.

Mason pulled me up off the floor, picked me up aggressively, and put me against the wall, kissing me so passionately. Mason pulled my dress up, and he entered inside of me

"Aghhhhhh ohhhhhh damn (panting)! Mason, Mason shittttttt with my hands wrapped tightly around his neck. His hands were grabbing my ass, pulling me up and down, creaming all over him until he exploded inside of me.

Pool Party flow

This mansion looks 12,000 sq ft fabulous three different pool areas, Jacuzzis, 12 bedrooms and 9.5 bathrooms, movie theater overlooking the ocean. The seating and bar area looked amazing. It was a cozy area with palm trees, and the night air feels amazing. The hookah girl came over and lit our hookah. We were relaxing and plotting. I told Mason I want to have him and another man fuck the shit out of me. He said he down and for me to set it up. I stopped this sexy ass papi from across the room, sitting at the bar drinking by himself. I excused myself from Mason and then approached the young gentlemen.

"Hello, is someone sitting here?"

"No, mami."

I ordered a drink, and the guy told the bartender to get me whatever I wanted.

Well, thank you. My name is Summer," I greeted, extending my hand.

He placed his soft lips, kissing my hand softly.

"My name is Juan. You are beautiful, Summer."

I placed my hands on his arm, lightly gazing them with a flirty touch.

We had some small talk for half an hour, and I told him how one of my fantasies is to have a MFM (male, female, male) session, especially with a Spanish man. He said he down to make it happen for me tonight.

We met up with Mason, who was now inside the mansion playing pool.

Both guys started playing each other and having small talk.

I walked over to Mason and started giving him head then, I called Juan over and then pulled his penis out. My eyes were wide, it was beautiful and fat. I gave him a nice hand job while still sucking Mason dick. I felt weird, but I had to live out this fantasy. Juan laid flat on the floor, and I sat on his face.

Mason stood over me, stroking his dick. While I sucked his balls, he slapped his penis on my forehead, and I leaned back, so he rubbed his dick all over my chest. I hopped up, ripped open the skyn condom, and slid it on Juan dick with my mouth. Then, my pussy tightly glided down his cock, and Mason stood tall and watched me ride his dick like I was in a rodeo.

Juan whispered in my ear, "Tu tener bueno la panocha" in Spanish, meaning *you have some good pussy.*

"Juan, I'm cummmmmmminnng, shit!"

I hopped up and gave him a golden shower. He opened his mouth wide and closed his eyes. Mason put me in doggy style position, and Juan stood up and sat on the pool table, and every pound Mason gave me, I put all that energy into giving Juan the best dick suck of his life. When his dick was in my throat, Mason pounded me harder.

Mason yelled, "You ready to catch our cum?"

I said, "Yesss!" as I dropped to my knees, opened my mouth, stuck my tongue out grab my titties, while Juan and Mason both stroked and shot cum all over me like a pearl necklace.

After we finished, I got Juan's phone number. I said to him, "Until we meet again."

Mason and I showered and headed back to the party.

* * *

The shenanigans going on outside was beyond wild. It was a huge female orgy with boobs and asses everywhere. A variety of sexy ladies were sucking, licking, fingering, and riding each other's faces.

We turned to my left, and it was there two sexy females, one Dominican and black, scissoring each other. It was the sexy shit ever. Their clits were rubbing intensely across each other. As I stood and watched, I couldn't help but masturbate from this live porn.

Mason French kissed me and rub on my boobs. This Caucasian women with these big titties started sucking on the other one. I looked over, and Mason began to moan so loud this thick ass BBW chocolate chick with small breasts and a tiny waist fat ass was sucking Mason manhood. This is the moment where my body lost control. I started mentally and physically shaking. This is the best orgasm ever.

Sam, an Asian female, put her fingers inside me while my volcano erupted all over her fingers, she focused on my g-spot rubbing in a circular motion. The party went on for the rest of the night while Mason and I watched the sunset while relaxing in a hammock.

CHAPTER 10

Birthday Party Flow

Tonight, I'll be celebrating my 27th birthday at Shades. My event is an all-white affair, for friends and family only guest list. My phone has been ringing nonstop since early this morning. I barely had the time to respond to everyone because I had so much running around to do. I have my mani/pedi appointment at noon, and luckily my 30-inch blonde wig was made last night. Tonight, I'll wear a sheer Chanel top and booty shorts with a gold bikini bra and panties. My gold strap sandals and gold bangles earrings would go perfect with my outfit.

* * *

Autumn arrived at my place around seven p.m. to get dressed for tonight. She wore a white Fendi dress and heels. We headed to Shades, where Paris and Bossy did an outstanding job with the decorations and glamour. At the club, they placed my diamond picture backdrop in the perfect spot. The DJ was setting up, and the liquor and sweets table looked amazing. I will be tending the bar for a couple hours to start everyone off the right way, and then one of the regulars bartenders will complete the shift. Mason hired a few exotic female dancers for my party, and Secret will also host. Everything was coming together pretty well — I knew my birthday party would be a success.

* * *

The club was starting to fill up, and around ten p.m. It was wall-to-wall and packed full of people. The DJ called me to the dance floor. It was time for me to twerk and make some birthday money. The bottled girls looked sexy in their two pieces as they flaunted, entertained, and passed out the Henny shots. Another stripper was dancing on the pool table, shaking her ass, and having a good time.

Everyone in the club screamed, "Happy Birthday, Summer!"

I sat in a chair in the middle of the floor, waiting for Secret to give me a sexy one-on-one dance. Mason rushed over, handed me a stack of cash, and I quickly tried to tuck it in my bra. City Girls started playing, and the ladies started twerking on men, shaking their ass, dancing, and shouting the lyrics ♪♪ *You tried it hoe, that shit ain't work. You made him bae, I fucked him first…*♪♪

My boo, Angela, looked super sexy in her tight and short white dress as it hugged her curves. Bossy and the team were in the building, and Bossy looked so good and original in her blinged-out dress. The diamonds on her dress were trimmed around her boob area, showing off her girls. Autumn's husband and girlfriend were in the building. I noticed that the crowd opened up a bit, and I saw Chef coming through with a triple-decker strawberry shortcake. He took whipped cream off the top, placed it on my lips, and kissed me softly.

Secret randomly came back over to pop her ass on me. I smacked her juicy ass and looked over at Angela. Angela walked over to me, stuck her tongue down my throat, and started rubbing my breasts. All three of us were fondling all over each other on the dance floor.

The DJ yelled over the microphone, "Summer, stay seated. You're about to get some more lap dances! Ladies, bring your sexy asses to the floor and show Summer a good time!"

The beat dropped, ♪♪ *Hot girl summer, so you know she got it lit…*♪♪

The crowd started going crazy. The first girl came over half-naked. She was a slim dark skin chick with a fat ass that she bounced and bounced. The crowd pulled their cameras out, recording every minute of it. Another bae came over and sat on top of me, rubbing me all sensual.

She whispered in my ear, saying she would be worth my while. She had really soft skin and was tall and slim. I had a big smile on my face. One of the guys started pouring Belaire Rose all over this big tittied girl.

We shut the club down tonight, and I was so lit that I barely could stand up. Secret gave me an ecstasy pill, and I was so horny and on cloud nine. For the entire night, I was the baddest bitch in the room.

* * *

My after-party was held at Pendulum. Now that it's three a.m., it's time for the real, freaky party to begin. I'm having an all-girl orgy, including Angela, Secret, and two baddies from the party. We sat around drinking, smoking, and getting acquainted. I let the ladies know that Sir Charles is in the building, and he may use the whips and vibrators tonight.

After a couple of drinks and dancing together, we started kissing, and I pulled out my nine-inch vibrating strap on, Big Pinky. One of the girls started sucking on it as if it were a real penis, and she looked really sexy doing it.

Her friend yelled out, "Can you stick it in my ass, please!"

They began to kiss and caress each other even more, and one thing led to another. I joined the fun and began to lick her nipples, and she was gently penetrated. Angela was next to us, laid on her back, enjoying getting eat out by Secret, and she devoured her pussy. Shortly after our girl time, Sir Charles finally arrived, and he had a nice, steamy session with everyone.

Secret experienced her first session of being spanked, and her ass turned so red. He did the erotic cupping method on Angela. She said it felt incredibly good on her skin.. It made her feel more sensitive. The other two ladies wanted to try the hot waxing. Everyone did this, and we took sexy pictures as well. They had other plans for me.

I was placed on the restrain cross and blindfolded and each lady could touch me anywhere on my body. They took turns. Somebody put the nipple calms on my breasts.

"Ouch," I replied.

I heard Secret say, "Shut up, Summer. I hope you're ready for this small bullet I'm going to place on your clit."

I was so high my body shiver from every touch. Angela kissed me all over my body. One of the females used electric shock rod chastity stimulates on me. The other female flogger my ass gently and then aggressive. This birthday night was very eventful.

* * *

Once I made it back home around six a.m., Mason was knocked out sleep. I laid on his chest and started rubbing the outside of his briefs. I bend over, hovering over his penis, and slowly woke his manhood up. He woke up still half-sleep and turned me over and scooped me up, both of us lying in the same direction, and thrust deep inside of me. The skin-to-skin contact made it so much better, and Mason put me right to sleep. He was still inside of me once we woke up.

CHAPTER 11

Miami

On the flight to Miami, Clark and I snuck to the bathroom, and he fucked me from the while back standing up. In this tight space, we were sweaty, and it was a lot of heavy breathing and electrifying passionate kissing. Wild spontaneous sex was something we always loved. I wasn't surprised when he told me to meet him in the restroom. After he lifted my skirt, I could feel his hard length entering my tight pussy. It was a quick fuck, but it was very intense due to the rush and suspense. After we both came, we quickly returned to first class. I ordered red wine and took a nice nap.

* * *

"Summer, we're here," Clark said. "I'm super excited for us to party with Jamal. He is here on business, and he was able to give us a complimentary upgrade on a room at the hotel".

Clark rented a bright orange Lamborghini Huracan Spyder, and people will definitely look twice when we ride past. After arriving at the hotel, we took showers, and Clark rolled a fat blunt.

I barely made it out of the shower, and he was all over me. His soft kisses touched every part of my body. I laid on my stomach as he arched my back and spread my ass apart. I then felt a warm sensation touch on my asshole as his tongue started gliding in and out slowly. My pussy started pulsating uncontrollably. He slid his fingers inside of me, and it sounded like someone was stirring up macaroni and cheese from all the wetness. I was getting more turned on by the minute, and the more I moaned, the harder he sucked.

I started yelling, "Stop Clark...Oooh, no, don't stop! I'm cummminng!"

He slurped, licked, and swallowed as I squirted, nearly drowning him with all of this clear fluid gushing out so strong at full force. I squirted straight in his face as if he were playing under a fire hydrant. Clark stood behind me and slid his big dick inside. He started off with a slow but consistent stroke, and his balls were hitting my clit. I squeezed my pussy tighter, and he increased the frequency of his stroke.

"AGHHHHH, SHIT! OH GOD, FUCK CLARK!" I gripped the sheets so tight that I almost broke a nail.

Clark dropped to his knees and slurped all my juices out of both holes. His hard rock dick started throbbing. He started grabbing my waist harder, and I moaned even more.

"Baby, bust all over my face!"

Clark held his dick while I got in position and opened wide with my tongue out. He released himself all in my mouth, and I closed my mouth on his dick so tight and swallowed every drop of his cum. The sex was so good, it almost put both of us to sleep.

* * *

Clark and I had plans, so we got dressed and head out for breakfast. After breakfast, we hit up stores on the strip and did a little shopping. I couldn't wait to put on my new two-piece white, silver, and diamonds stub bikini. The air smelled so fresh, and the beach water was so clear. I loved the perfect, clean sand between my toes. This was just the vacation I needed. Clark looked sexy with his white swim trunks, and his thick, dick print pierced through the fabric. He is tall with a dark chocolate skin tone and an athletic build.

Once we found a comfortable spot to lounge and relax, we rented a tent and chairs. We sat at the bar for a while and ordered an appetizer and drinks. After relaxing on the beach and smoking, we went jet skiing. I only got on once in my life, and I was so scared to try it again. Clark told me to get on with him and then try it on my own once I was comfortable. After the first 20 minutes of flowing across the waters, I was ready to run circles around him.

Once we got back on the beach, we smoked again and took a quick nap under the shady tent. We spent the rest of the day relaxing on the beach, and when the sun started going down, Clark grabbed my hand and led me to the water. He sat down, and I sat on top of him, grinding him so hard until he got an erection. I slid my bikini to the side and rode him. He grabbed my ass, helping me rock back and forth. I placed my hands on his face, and tongue kissed him so passionately. I was in heaven at the moment with not a care in the world. After about fifteen minutes of sex on the beach, we stopped and cleaned our things to head back to the hotel.

* * *

I wore a two-piece tan skirt set from Fashion Nova and red bottoms. Clark is wearing a button-down Paisley short set with his white Alexander McQueen sneakers. We drove 45 minutes to the strip club. The line was long, but because of my brother Rudolph's connections, we could go to the side for VIP entry. I had a bag full of money, and I was ready to get lit and turn up.

We saw Jamal and his crew in another VIP section with sexy women surrounding them, twerking their asses and pussy. I got right in the mix and started dancing too, then suddenly the dancer on the pole called me to the stage.

"Come to the stage, Summer! It's ya muthafucking birthday!" The stripper was on the pole and asked me to sit on her and twirled me around the pole while sitting on her legs. When I stood up, she asked me to rub icing all over her ass. I added sprinkles, and she took a sparkler so that I could light it. Her soft ass was like a big chocolate birthday cake...I blew out the sparkler as if I made a wish. I twerked while licking the icing off, and the crowd went wild. Clark helped me off the stage, and we started taking more shots of Henny. Ass was poppin', money was being thrown in the air, and we partied until three a.m.

* * *

Afterwards, Jamal took Clark and me to an underground strip club where it was nothing but Cuban and Colombian women. They were perfect looking and flawless. Jamal gave everyone a stack and told us to ball out and have fun. We saw this 5'5 caramel complexioned Cuban woman with soft, dark brown hair hanging to her lower back, cut in layers. She had brown hair with blonde highlights. Her breasts sat so perfectly, her waist was so fit and small, and her ass was fat and round.

The women looked so beautiful, and I was like a kid in a candy store. She told me that her name was Jasiel. We chatted for a bit, sipped, and opened up to one another. Clark and I invited Jasiel to the private room, and we had a threesome. I couldn't stop cumming, and I was so turned the entire time. Her mouth and soft, plump lips felt so warm and amazing. After we finished, Clark and I headed back to the hotel to get some rest to prepare for our flight the next afternoon.

CHAPTER 12

Wild Work Week

I was finally back home after a wonderful weekend with Clark. This afternoon I'll be doing Chef's yearly inspection at his restaurant, and I told my boss I'd be doing this by myself. Once I arrived at the restaurant, Chef told me to wait in the front lobby. He greeted me with a hug and kiss and asked me to turn around so that he could blindfold me. The aroma in the air smelled exquisite. We walked into the main dining area, and he took off the blindfold, and there were colorful flowers everywhere.

"Happy belated birthday, baby," Chef said proudly. It was a beautiful candlelit lunch for two.

"Chef, it looks amazing, and yesss, I'm starving," I stated while giving him a hug and kiss. He made a spread of lobster, steak with mushrooms, onions and peppers, mashed potatoes, and asparagus.

"You are such a ladies man. You know exactly how to put a big smile on my face."

"Well, Summer...I missed you very much."

We talked for a while, to catch up on the new things we had going on. The food tasted so delicious. He leaned across the table and planted a big kiss on my lips. He led me to the kitchen area, pulled my shirt up, lifted me on the counter, and grabbed my ass so tight. We started kissing, and our tongues were doing the tango. His aggressiveness turned me on. He placed his hands under my shirt and massaged my pussy. He whispered in my ear, letting me know that he could tell I'm not wearing any underwear. I instantly got wet, moaned softly, and then he kissed my neck so passionately.

The smell of his Versace cologne drove me wild. I was so soaking wet because the energy was so intense. He started kissing me from head to toe, licking every part of my body. Once he made it to my toes, he placed them in his mouth while rubbing his hands up and down my thighs and legs. He kissed his way up my legs and into my inner thighs. He blew a soft blow to my vagina and had an admiring look in his eyes.

"Summer, baby ya pussy is so pretty," Chef said.

I felt a warm sensation as his mouth covered my pussy.

I closed my eyes enjoying every moment of pleasure. I began to rub on my breast and held his head with my right hand. I started to gyrate my pussy until I released my juices all over his face. He asked me to stand up and he bend me over the counter and we fucked for the next two hours throughout the entire restaurant.

Ladies Night

Autumn, Paris, Angela, Bossy, and I will be hitting the streets tonight. We have reservations at Chef's restaurant, and then we'll go dancing at a club downtown. I had pretty close relationships with all of my girls. Autumn and I always had a tight relationship growing up, and there was never any competition among us. We both were introduced to the lifestyle in our college years in Atlanta. We were always spontaneous and open with our sexuality. Autumn met her fiancé at a party during her sophomore year in school; and their senior year, they met their girlfriend. I met Bossy while she was hosting a lifestyle party at one of the fraternity dorms during my freshman year. I met Clark that same night, we caught each other's attention immediately, and we have been friends ever since.

Bossy was a great person to know. She was well-known and respected throughout school, and she was a senior when we met. She was an entrepreneur and ran a private escort business. When Autumn and I needed extra money, Bossy would arrange us on dates with wealthy men. A lot of men were looking for sugar babies, and they would wine and dine us and cater to our personal expenses. There were also a few kinky men who would have different types of fetishes, which would not necessarily involve sex.

A year after Bossy's graduation from college, one of her sugar daddies moved her close to Philadelphia, and she now lives in a small mansion outside of the city.

Paris and I met at Mason's club five years ago. She had such a big vibrant personality. When the song that sang "Watch Out For The Big Girls" played, Paris pushed everyone out of the way and held her own on the dance floor. She was pretty popular, and she sells sex toys and lingerie. Paris also was a BBW dominatrix at night and a second-grade school teacher during the day. I met Angela three years ago when Clark introduced us at a party. Angela and I had similar personalities. We clicked right away and have been close ever since.

* * *

It's about 9pm, and we were running a little behind schedule. Autumn and I arrived first, and Paris, Bossy, and Angela were trailing not far behind. Once we all were seated, the waiter filled our glasses with water, and there was a bottle of expensive wine chilled on our table. The waiter let us know that the chef would be out to help us, and we sat patiently and talked about our day.

"Hello ladies, welcome to my restaurant. I'll be serving Chef's choice options. On the menu, we have duck, veil, lobster, steak, or fish. For sides, the options are mashed potatoes, rice medley, baked sweet potato, steamed broccoli, sautéed brussel sprouts, or fresh string beans. You ladies also can choose between a side soup or salad to compliment your meal," he explained.

I introduced Chef to all the ladies. Everyone gave him sweet compliments, and he humbly blushed at all the love he was receiving. He bent down, gave me a kiss on the cheek, and told us that the waiter will take our order and if we need anything to let him know.

As we waited for our meal, I told the ladies about my sexual afternoon work visit with him. Bossy laughed and said, "I bet you had a good time, Summer."

* * *

After we all ate, we stayed at Chef's restaurant until almost eleven p.m. We all were stuffed, and the food was amazing. Once we were ready, we said thank you and goodbye to Chef; now it was time to have a ladies night of fun.

We arrived at a club by midnight and partied hard for a few hours. We all then checked out the after-hour strip club that Secret works at. I called Mason and told him to meet me in the parking lot when he closed the lounge. While waiting for Mason in the parking lot of the club, my homegirl Christine was calling me.

"Hey, Christine!" I said. I was so happy to hear from her.

"Hey, boo, I have a crazy story to tell you," Christine replied.

"Okay...I'm listening. Are you cool? It's pretty late," I questioned.

"Well, today I was hanging out with my ex, Sharif...when I arrived at his house, my phone rang on my car's Bluetooth. I answered, and a woman was on the other end, but I didn't recognize her voice. That's when I realized that Sharif's phone must've automatically synced to the Bluetooth in my car once I pulled up. She asked for him, and I questioned her and found out she has been around since last year. I lied...I told her that he was my husband and not to call him anymore," Christine describes.

"Oh, really...wow. Well, what did Sharif say? Does he know?" I asked.

"Girl, I was pissed. She hung up the phone on me. Eventually, he came out of the house, and I just left him where he stood," she explained.

"Wow...these men," I replied to Christine.

"But that's not the crazy story I called to tell you. So, earlier today, my electricity was acting up. I called the electric company, asked them to send a technician out, and they set an appointment for eight p.m. Well, eight o'clock passed, and no one showed up. I went to take my bath, and around the time I was done, the doorbell rang, so I rushed and ended up answering in my robe.

I opened the door, and I was speechless. The electrician was so fine. I told him to come in, and when he walked passed me, I noticed that he smelled amazing. He asked me what was wrong, and I could barely get my words together. I took him to the circuit breaker in the basement, and I noticed that he was eyeing me. I told him that I loved his cologne. He thanked me and told me that he loved my smell too!" Christine said in excitement.

"So, what happened next?"

"We started making small talk, and I noticed he kept staring at me. Bitch, the next thing you know, we started kissing! He pushed me up against the washing machine, lifted me off my feet, and sat me on top of it. I started unbuttoning his clothes. He was nice and cut...he had very nice muscles and smooth skin. I started to rub all over his arms and chest. He pulled me to the edge of the washer and started fucking the shit out of me, Summer!" Christine shared.

"Ooohh, so you did something spontaneous? Not little miss goody two shoes," I sarcastically said while laughing.

"Lord knows I needed that! Since Sharif has been out of the picture, I haven't had any. We just got finish fucking...that's why I had to call and tell you! I'll call you later today," Christine expressed.

"Okay, girl. Mason will be here soon. Hit me up later," I said before hanging up the phone. I was both surprised and happy that Christine finally decided to let her guard down to have some wild sexy fun.

* * *

Once he arrived, Mason and I entered the club, and the lights were flashing everywhere. I walked over to my friends who already were drinking, partying, and throwing ones and fives in the air. Bossy told Mason and me that we made it just in time because Secret was coming up next. Trey Songz featuring Nicki Minaj's "Bottoms Up" started playing, and Secret's sexy ass walked to the stage with a multicolored netted bodysuit and hot pink stilettos. She walked around the pole seductively, climbed up the pole, and then came down slowly like she was riding a bike. Once she reached the bottom and hit the stage, she dropped right into a split. Secret was so sexy whenever she performed, and I admired her confidence and sex appeal.

CHAPTER 13

Complete Stranger

After a long day of work, it's time to finally end the last flight for the day. I decided to get a drink and something to eat inside the airport before heading home. I sat at one end of the bar, and a man was looking at me from the other side of the bar. I didn't pay him too much mind as I ordered my food and focused on my phone.

As I was taking a selfie, the gentleman walked over to me and asked if he could see it. He introduced himself as "the man I need to get to know". He was very straightforward. He told me how pretty I looked, complimented my smile, and insisted on buying me a drink. I told him that I've seen him a few times around the airport, and he admitted to recognizing me previously, but he preferred to wait for the perfect opportunity to approach me.

I was enjoying our conversation and connection. The way he looked at me was driving me wild inside. The thought of pleasing him and his mysteriousness made me excited. Tonight, may just be his lucky night because Mason is away on business.

After we finished our round of drinks, the gentleman asked if we could go back to his place and chill. I agreed, and we made our way. As we got on the highway, I realized that he didn't live far from Angela. I texted her info about the gentleman, my whereabouts, and let her know that I was up to one of my shenanigans.

His house was really nice on a quiet block in the northeast. The inside was even more appealing. It had mirrors all over the living-room wall, nice big brown leather furniture, and a color scheme of earth tone colors, green, and tan. He had a minibar in the dining room area with top-shelf drinks and wine on the counters.

We continued to talk as he gave me a tour of his home, and he expressed how he was mesmerized by my beauty and intrigued by my personality. We made it to his bedroom, where a huge king-sized bed was placed. It looked really comfortable with beautiful bed covers. His master bathroom had a gorgeous chrome sink, stand-in shower, and jacuzzi whirlpool tub.

I looked over at him, and I noticed that he was undressing me with his eyes, and he asked if he could kiss me. I instantly tingled down below as he leaned in and kissed me softly. I started unbuttoning his shirt. He was small framed with tight muscles and about six feet tall. I was ready to get down to business and unwrap his present. The level of energy flowing through the room was unreal.

Once I unbuckled his pants, I was pleased with my gift for tonight. I slowly planted soft wet kisses around his penis, and he instantly started growing in my mouth. I continued to kiss it slowly as my saliva built up more and more. The thick presence felt good in my mouth. He began to moan, and I sucked harder and tighter. I opened up wide, stuck my tongue out, and allowed it to go deep down my throat. I held onto him, and he gripped my head so tight and yelled my name. He was so far down my vocals that I started humming, and I used my tongue to massage his balls. I bobbed my head back and forth, jerked my head, and locked my lips on his dick. The intensity was increasing, and his moan got louder and louder until he exploded in my mouth. I opened wide, with my tongue out as his creamy fluid was released. He gave me a nice facial, and I finished him as I sucked every drop out.

He laid out, relaxed on the bed, and appeared to be in shock from what just happened.

After fifteen minutes of silence, I returned to the bedroom, and he asked me to come sit on his face, so I lifted my thick thighs over his face. He placed one hand on my ass and the other hand on my breasts as I rocked back and forth like I was riding a horse. I grind my pussy on his tongue, and my juices released from my body. After I climbed off, he said he was ready for round two. I noticed his soldier was still at attention, so I eased myself on top, slowly grind up, down, back and forth, rocking my hips. He sucked and licked both breasts, and my eyes rolled toward the back of my head. I hopped on my feet and started bouncing. I was riding him like I was in the Kentucky Derby. He placed his hands around my waist, and his strength allowed me to stay in rhythm. In mid-air I squirted out like Niagara Falls over his stomach and linen sheets. He lifted me off of him, threw me on the bed, looked me in my eyes, and asked was I ready for more.

He placed my legs inside his torso in a pretzel position and set my feet together against his chest. He slid his hard dick inside of my pussy, and I felt my tightness give in, even though I was soaking wet. He started slow stroking my pussy. It felt like his cock was playing peek-a-boo with my g-spot. He moved at a controlled pace, and I released my muscles as I inhaled and exhaled. I started cumming so hard! He held my face, made me look him in his eyes, and kissed me aggressively. I couldn't believe that this complete stranger had me so open.

* * *

Last night was so amazing, and the unreal connection was remarkable. I replayed every moment in my head while lying in my bed. The amount of pleasure he possessed over my body was indescribable. He was able to meet my entire sexual desire, and I needed it after my long week. That night of passionate sex calmed my soul.

I received a text from my mystery man.

Mystery Man: *Summer, I had an amazing time with you last night. I hope you felt the same way, and I hope to see you again...please don't be a stranger.*

CHAPTER 14

Hawaiian Festival

The entire hotel is shut down for a full-fledged, fun extravaganza. The festivities and activities are set for two nights and three days of action. For most of the stay, you can choose to participate or not. Everyone is coming at night, and hosts and party promoters are expecting over five hundred guests. These swinger events happen about twice a year. An entire hotel is usually rented or reserved for specific guests of the event. Many rooms are designated for certain situations, including a smoking room, BDSM room, pegging room, vendor room, and a room you can buy food, edibles, and alcoholic beverages in, etc.

The hotel's ballroom is where the main event is held tonight. This is where everyone comes together in one enormous space to dance, drink, and turn up. This year has a sex Hawaiian theme, and the women will most likely be wearing bathing suits, straw skirts, and coconut breasts. The main events eventually turn into fuck fests, and partygoers can play in their personal rooms or any discreet place they chose.

Mason, Angela, Secret, and I are staying in the same room. We have a spacious king suite with a jacuzzi whirlpool tub in the bathroom. The bedroom was huge, and I couldn't wait to cuddle up with Mason and my girls after our night of fun.

After getting dressed, I walked through the hotel areas to see what the vibe was so far. The DJ is set up outside near the hotel's outdoor pool. The large jacuzzi was full of topless women —ass and titties were everywhere. Men were lusting all over the women, and everyone was all smiles. It was nothing but good vibes and great energy at the event, and I couldn't wait to see how the night would end.

Once my friends arrived, I knew shit would just get started.

Bossy: *I'm wearing my floral, two-piece bikini with a sheer wrap. I invited a new guy that I met from New York, and I was excited to bring him around. I even bought all of my toys with me tonight. I'm feeling really kinky and wouldn't mind tying up a fine ass man.*

Autumn: *Finally, time to check in. Next, I'm going to change and get sexy. Where is everyone at?*

Derrick: *I'm taking a nap, and I'll meet up with you guys later.*

Tonya: *I can't wait to wear my see-through bikini set. It's party and turn up time!*

Paris: *I'm all set up to make some extra money this weekend. My cousin will be selling some of my lingerie sets. Now all I have to do is fuck shit up! I plan on fucking and getting loose this weekend. I have to find the BDSM room, and I plan on getting spanked.*

Kiesha: *Jamal, Jane, and I are all set up to have an orgy tonight. We have to find some sexy ladies willing to get down and nasty.*

Jane: *I set the toys and wipes on our dresser. Kiesha and I should have a quick session together before we meet up with everyone.*

Jamal: *I can't wait to spank Kiesha and Jane's ass tonight! We are exhibitionists, so I'll be leaving our room door wide open for anyone who wants to see a show!*

Clark: *I have this leather leash that I plan to tie on Erica. She's been a bad girl. She needs to be trained.*

Erica: *I love it when Clark dominates me. I just want to get on my knees and please him.*

After I got dressed and put on my favorite perfume, I headed to the ballroom to attend the main event. Everyone was smiling, connecting, and interacting. This event was an environment where guests can be free sexual beings in a no-judgment zone.

I looked to my left, and people were kissing. Over to my right people were taking photos. I saw so many familiar faces and greeted them with hugs and kisses. We line-danced, twerked, gave lap dances, mingled, and drank the entire night.

Around four a.m., people started going their separate ways. Mason, Angela, Secret, and I found another couple to join us in our room, and we all fucked until eight a.m. The guy was a fine, tall, and light skin gentleman named Dom. His lady was short, petite, and mixed. Her name was Kandy.

Mason enjoyed Kandy. He had her bent over, stretched out, and picked up as he fucked her in different positions. I played with Angela using a big pink strap on, and Dom was fucking Secret from the back. Every female took turns giving the men head, and the men also took turns sucking and licking our pussies — we all were satisfied. We had a freaky choo-choo train orgy, a few hours of nonstop fucking, sucking, and licking.

* * *

I woke up around noon, took a shower, and went outside of the hotel building to relax and enjoy the early afternoon breeze. While I was sitting there, a couple randomly approached me, asking if they could taste me as I was laid back in the chair. I agreed to the offer, and the man took the pineapples that I was eating and squeezed some of the juices on my stomach. The pineapple juice dripped right down to my vagina. The woman got on her knees and used her tongue to lick every drop off of me.

I softly moaned as she licked my pussy. Her mouth felt so good, and her lips were soft. I loved how gentle she was as she massaged my clit with her tongue. They took turns in giving me oral pleasure. The male partner pulled me closer to his mouth, grabbed my thighs, and sucked my clitoris so tight. He had a gap in his front teeth, which felt so sensitive, tingly, and good on my clit. He took his tongue and flickered it up and down so fast.

As the woman sucked my breasts and he continued to lick my clit in a fast pace, I orgasmed. My legs shook as I continued to cum in his mouth. The man slurped and licked his lips while the woman moaned; after the couple finished pleasing me, they thanked me and said they enjoyed the moment and lifestyle event even more.

Afterward, I headed back to the room to freshen up, but before I got to my room door, Clark spotted me and pulled me into his room. Erica was lying on their room's sofa while wearing a silk, red robe. They both looked so sexy, and I automatically thought of Clark's ability to make me have multiple orgasms and squirt. I fucked up all of their sheets while we fucked. I watched him fuck Erica on their bed after I squirted for the second time, and he power drilled the shit out of her. Clark and Erica were so aggressive together, and I loved watching how passionately they fucked.

* * *

Back at the suite, Angela was still asleep, and the other couple left. Mason and Secret were having some fun. He was using the wand on her pussy, and she was going crazy. I brought some fruit up to the room since Secret recently mentioned that she wanted to have some fun with grapefruit. I took the fruit to the kitchen area, cut a hole in the middle, and warmed it up in water, so that Secret and I can use it on Mason's dick.

I entered the bedroom where they were playing, and as soon as Secret saw the grapefruit, her eyes lit up. Mason stood in front of us, and she placed the warm grapefruit around his penis, squeezed it, and stroked back and forth while she sucked him dry. We both took turns sucking his big dick, and it tasted so good with the fruit juices dripping all over it. Mason's legs got stiff, and Secret continued to suck harder and apply more pressure. Mason released himself, I removed the grapefruit, stuffed his manhood down my throat, and swallowed the rest. Secret and I tongue kissed as Mason relaxed out on the bed.

* * *

64

The last party of the event was just getting started. The hosts arranged a Hawaii style buffet along with a hula dance show. I met so many different singles and couples at the buffet dinner. There was a variety of people from the west coast, east coast, Midwest, and so on. The outdoor pool was full, and the twerk contest was starting. Secret was a part of the twerk contest, and with the ass and skills she has, she should win.

The crowd gathered and chanted as the sexy women twerked for the $300 prize. Secret shook her ass to the beat of the song, twerked on her knees, and ended with a full split. My girls and I celebrated Secret's win for the rest of the night and partied until the sun came up.

CHAPTER 15

Houston, Texas

I felt the sun beaming on my skin and sweat dripping off my skin. I was so happy to be out of the city with Mr. Biggam for another weekend. It's been some time since I've seen him, but we made sure that we FaceTime throughout the week. Biggam still has been consistent with sending roses to my job and keeping a smile on my face.

We first arrived at his family's ranch house. Once we entered the driveway, I noticed the beautiful horses and cows in the barnyard. The architecture was exquisite. From the exterior to the interiors, everything was incredibly detailed. I felt welcomed by his sister, who was waiting for our arrival. Biggam introduced me to his sister, and she gave me a tour of their fabulous family home. The kitchen had french oak wood cabinets and stainless-steel appliances, the fireplace in the living room was so cozy, and the walls were stone throughout the long hallways. My favorite part was the view of the outdoor pool from the patio doors.

The ranch house had a modern but vintage style. The wooden steps led us to the master suite that Biggam and I will be staying for the next couple of days. The bedroom was huge, with a leather, tan king-sized bedroom room set. The suite was also filled with a multicolored plush rug, two nightstands, a chest dresser, a sofa loveseat, and a 60-inch mounted flat screen TV. The master bathroom had two sinks with a floor rug shaped like the state of Texas. The tub was an antique white with stainless steel knobs. The ranch had five oversized bedrooms, four bathrooms, a laundry room, and a sunroom.

After the tour, Biggam took me to see the horses in the barnyard. Once we got over there, I noticed a beautiful black stallion named Jesus. I held Biggam's and so tight because I was a little nervous. He assured me that I was safe and kissed me on my lips. I got so turned on that touching turned into sucking. The next thing you know, I felt hay in my ass while he was eating my pussy. I grabbed the back of his head and arched back as my juices released all in his mouth. I hopped up and rode him like I was in a rodeo. When he started sucking on my titties, I began to cum and screamed so loud. I felt the build-up and thickness in Biggam's dick, and right before he was about to explode, I rode him in reverse cowgirl position. My ass clapped and bounced against his sweaty abs. We both reached climax and came together.

After our sex in the barnyard, we were still full of energy and decided to take a shower and get dressed. Biggam wanted to take me into town for dinner and go dancing. Being with him was a breath of fresh air. We had an amazing night together. We danced in our cowboy boots, ate dinner, had a few drinks, and talked about how we enjoy each other's company.

"I wish I could see you more. You keep me young," Biggam stated.

"Yes, big daddy! My time with you is always fun," I replied with a smile.

* * *

The next morning, Biggam woke me up with so much enthusiasm with plans to go out in the city to have fun in the sun.

"Close your eyes, baby girl," he said to me. "Surprise! Your very own cowboy hat!"

"It looks fabulous on me, thank you so much," I expressed him while giving him a kiss.

I wanted to be stylish but comfortable today with all the walking we have planned, so I wore my fitted, cream Chanel dress and my Chanel sneakers.

Biggam and I went to breakfast and then to the downtown aquarium. We also went to the Houston Museum District and the local zoo. I enjoyed the flamingos and bird exhibits the most. After sightseeing and visiting a few historic spots, Biggam and I went back to the house to freshen up and change outfits for our evening plans. We finished our night off at Kemah Boardwalk near the waterfront. We rode the Ferris wheel, and he couldn't keep his hands off of me. We kissed and hugged onto each other most of the ride.

* * *

The next day was Sunday, and it was my last day here in Texas. I sat on the edge of the bed, thinking of how much fun I had for the past few days with Biggam.

"I'm exhausted, big daddy." I sighed.

"Aye, Summer, are you too tired for a mall run?" he asked.

I jumped up with excitement and said, "Hell no, I'm not!"

I packed my suitcase and got dressed for my last day here in Texas. Biggam and I went to Memorial City Mall, and it was enormous. There was a movie theater, ice skating venue, and over 150 stores for shopping. He took me to Saks Fifth Avenue and bought me a red Louis Vuitton bag. He also told me to pick out as many outfits, shoes, and accessories as I'd like. We had so many bags that we had to make trips to the car to avoid walking around the mall with too many items.

* * *

After shopping, we ate lunch at the local food court and then went to the theater to watch a movie. We saw a film full of sex scenes, and every time an intimate scene played, I was aroused. I knew that I wasn't gonna see my big daddy in a while, so I took advantage of the moment. I took my hand and placed it on his thigh and rubbed his thigh. He glanced at me with a smirk as I smiled back at him. I peeked around the theater to make sure it was fairly empty and lowered my head to give him slow but steady head. I lifted my head and surveyed the room one more time. I slipped up my skirt, stood up, planted my feet, and straddled his big dick. I bounced up and down on his cock, closed my eyes, and then went to another place. I was no longer in that theater. I was in ecstasy. I rode that chocolate dick until he let go of his heavy load and came all inside my tight pussy. I loved the warmth of his cum inside of me. This was the going away present I needed. I need Biggam to think of me until the next time we meet.

CHAPTER 16

Lingerie Party

This night it's going to be epic. It's been a month and a half since I've seen everyone. Tonight, I'll be getting super sexy in my black with two-piece lace lingerie set with wings. I purchased it from Paris' lingerie collection earlier this week. I brought a nice mask to cover my face, and I'll be wearing my red bottoms. I can't wait to see everyone tonight.

Autumn: *What am I going to wear tonight? My sister is going to kill me if my outfit is not on point. I'm happy that my fiancee and our girlfriend will be attending this party with me. I just hope that I can find something super cute at the mall for tonight.*

Mr. Chef: *I'm cooking my ass off for the Lingerie Masquerade Party. I have my waiter uniform ready, and my workers will be on point — I need everyone to represent my company well. Tonight's menu will consist of bacon-wrapped buffalo shrimp, oysters, stuffed mushrooms, bacon macaroni and cheese bites, Greek salad bites, cocktail shrimp, and small plates of salad. Each person will have a main course choice of salmon or chicken with their meal.*

Angela: *My hair is almost done, and then I can relax before this evening. I just got a Brazilian wax, manicure, and pedicure. I'll be wearing a sexy sheer, hot pink lingerie set with my colorful mask. My ass will look so right! can't wait to see my babe Summer and have a lil fun tonight.*

Bossy: *The team and I will be in the building representing New Jersey. I have some running around to do, but not much. I have a purple bodysuit that I'll be wearing tonight and my shimmery mask with the feathers coming out of it.*

Jamal: *I'm at the mall trying to find a nice outfit to wear tonight. I'm thinking maybe some silk pajamas that show my dick print when it's rock hard. The ladies love that. Or perhaps I should keep it simple and wear some colorful Ethika boxers. I can't wait to see all the sexy women tonight in their lingerie...it'll be ass everywhere!*

Paris: *The ladies are going to look good tonight. I can't believe I sold out most of my lingerie outfits. I sell lingerie for all sizes, including petite, medium, and BBW. So, I know that everyone will come through looking great in their pieces! I have a custom-made leopard catsuit for tonight, and I can't wait to wear it and take pictures with my girls.*

* * *

The place looks great! The party planner did an excellent job of bringing my vision to life. The DJ is ready, and Chef is all set up looking super good in his uniform. Paris recommended that someone stay at the front lobby to collect the money and put the wristbands on. So now, we're patiently waiting until nine p.m. for the doors to open.

At nine p.m. sharp, guests started pouring in, and everyone looked magnificent, dressed to impress. I was greeting the guests and showed everyone where to find drinks, food, and restrooms. After security came into place, it became my time to mingle and have fun.

"Hello, gorgeous," a deep voice spoke to me from behind.

I turned around, and it was Clark. "Hey baby, so which one of your ladies did you bring out tonight?"

"Kim is over there checking out some lingerie from Paris' table," he said while pointing.

"Okay, great. Have fun, thanks for coming. Bossy should be pulling up soon. You know she is always running late," I explained.

* * *

The party was finally packed, and the dance floor was crowded. Everyone was getting drunk, dancing, and having a great time.

I ran into Jamal, and he looked confused and lost.

"Where is she at? I have yet to lay my eyes on her because everyone is wearing a mask, and I can't tell which one she is," Jamal said while looking around.

"Hey, bestie, what's wrong?" I asked.

"I'm looking for your sister," Jamal replied.

"Ohhhh, okay. She is standing over there. Do you see anyone dressed in the peacock colors and with the feathers coming out her mask?" I quizzed.

"Ohhh, yes! I see her. I see her. I'll catch you later," he said with excitement.

Moments later, Autumn rushed over to me with a big smile.

"Summer! You would not believe what just happened. Jamal just ate my pussy in the bathroom," she said in a shocked, whisper tone.

"Both of you are freaks and would make a dope ass team," I said to her with a smile.

* * *

The Masquerade Lingerie Party was a lot of fun. We had a best-dressed contest, and Angela won. Her makeup looked really well and matched her lingerie outfit. Her body looked so well in it, and her ass was so juicy in the thong piece. Secret danced most of the night and danced on the majority of the men and women. Men threw money in the air for all the ladies who danced and twerked at the event. Everyone smoked blunts and drank the best liquor. It was nothing but sexiness and good vibes.

* * *

The party ended, and a few cleaners were wrapping things up as we were headed out. Chef agreed to take Angela and me home, and on the ride back, I started to give him head while he was driving. Once we arrived, I invited him to come up and play with us. We made it upstairs, relaxed, and took a few shots. I played music, and that's when the magic began.

I sat, looked at both of them, and said, "Now this is my perfect poly."

The three of us made love, and the chemistry was so real. Chef, Angela, and I mesh so well sexually and personally. Chef took his time with me and gave me a full body massage. He also gave Angela a massage, rubbing down every part of her part. He ate my pussy so good, and I came in less than five minutes while Angela sucked on my nipples. I decided to make a video because I wanted this moment to last forever.

The way Chef was eating Angela was so aggressive, and she was in a zone. He stuck his finger inside of her tight pussy and massaged her g-shot in a circular motion as I kissed her passionately. He turned her over, and I laid on my back while he stroked her in and out repeatedly with his thumb in her ass. Chef smacked her on her ass as she moaned while sucking on my dripping wet pussy. He came inside of her warmness, and we all climaxed together. Angela was fucked so good by Chef that she went into the other room and passed out.

I started sucking his dick, and he went crazy. I laid on my back while we made love in the missionary position for the next hour. We gazed into each other's eyes and soaked in every second.

Chef whispered, "I want you to have my baby, Summer. I love you!" he moaned so loud, and then I felt a gush of warm nut flow inside of my pussy. He held me tight, and as his body trembled and legs shook while he released every bit of sperm inside my pussy.

CHAPTER 17

Holidays

Thanksgiving came fast, and the year is almost over. Tonight, I planned to make my rounds to visit family and friends. Tomorrow night I'll be hosting a small get-together at Mason's place, and I need it to be really perfect. Mason's mother, sister, and brother are also town for the holidays. My brother Rudolph will be coming to dinner, which I'm so happy about because he works so hard, and Autumn and I barely get to see him.

My sister and I have to cook Jamaican and Spanish dishes as well. We will have turkey, ham, stuffing, yams, macaroni and cheese, potato salad, rice, collard greens, jerk chicken, dumplings, oxtail, paella, prawns in fried garlic, plantain, and soft homemade dinner rolls. Mason's mother will be bringing cassava leaf and fish. We more than covered enough nationalities with our around the world cuisines.

"It's time to get dressed, Autumn. Did you talk to our mommy, daddy, or Rudolph?" I asked her.

"Yes, they are on their way now," she responded.

I was so excited just thinking about seeing my big brother and parents. I rushed to the shower to get prepared for my family and friends gathering.

"Is that the doorbell, Mason? Can you get that please?" I shouted.

"Yes, babe!" he yelled back.

"Hey!!! Mom, I miss you. Hi Tracy, Marie, and Mike. I miss you guys. Aww, look at my nieces and nephews," Mason said as he greeted his family with love.

More guests filled the home, and Autumn and I rushed to get ready to head downstairs. There was football playing on the television in the man cave room, soft music playing from the speaker, wine served for adults and toys out for the kids. We had something for everyone to be entertained with as we waited for the guests and food to finish. Once everyone arrived, it was time to bless the food and say what we were thankful for.

Everyone was satisfied and happy with tonight's gathering — the food was perfect, and everyone was delighted. Mason and I thanked everyone for coming, and we rapped the night up with kisses and hugs to our family and friends as they left. Afterward, Angela and I cleaned up the entire house while Mason left to go to the club to shut it down by two a.m. After this long day, I thought about having some sexy fun tonight when he got back home.

"I missed you guys. The last time I've seen y'all was two days after the lingerie party, and we had a threesome," I said when Mason got back home.

Angela and I were lying in bed comfortably, and I reached over, grabbed her hand, and placed it on my pussy so she could feel how wet I've gotten thinking about our last two encounters. Mason rushed to the shower, and I think he knew what he was about to get into. While he showered, Angela and I kissed and licked on each other until Mason was ready to give us his big dick.

When Mason was finished, he grabbed the baby oil and rubbed it on my ass. Angela started sucking on my titties and rubbed my pussy softly. Mason turned the music, lit some candles, and the mood was set.

Mason stood in front of Angela, and she started sucking his dick nice and slow. I joined and began rubbing his balls. We started French kissing all over his manhood. I laid on my back while they both took turns eating, sucking, and slurping my pussy juices.

I told Angela to lay on her back. It was now her turn to get her pussy sucked. She tasted like fresh spring water, and Mason and I couldn't get enough. I told her to sit on my face while Mason is fucking me. As she sat on my face, Mason continued to penetrate me and suck on her boobs. They kissed, and next thing you know, Angela and I climaxed at the same time. I gushed and squirted all over the place. Angela and I switched positions so that she can get some dick. Mason pounded her from the back while she was eating me out. The harder he fucked her, the better the head felt. Eventually, the three of us came together. Mason sat up, and Angela turned around quickly so that he could cum all over our faces.

Angela buried her face in my pussy gripped her head tight while I called out his name and asked him how her pussy felt. The sensation build up my grip got tighter, and she was unable to catch her breath. I exploded all over her face screaming, "Oh Mason, ohhhhh Mason! Yessss, baby! I'm cumming!"

Then we locked eyes, and to my surprise, he yelled, "I'm about to bust! Oh, shit!" Mason held his big dick, trying to control his nut and told her to turn around and he cream pie all over her face.

* * *

I was expecting ten ladies and ten men for my Friendsgiving Potluck night. I planned a night full of liquor, home-cooked meals, and games. The ladies were instructed to bring a dish, and the fellas were told to supply alcohol and marijuana. The party started at ten o'clock, and the first game to play was called Eat the Pie. The ladies had to lay on the floor with towels, and the fellas had to select a lady and what kind of pie they preferred. They then placed the pie on top of the woman's vagina, and the first one to eat the pie wins.

Couple number one is Jane and Jamal.
Couple number two is Paris and Rudolph.
Couple number three is Angela and Dre.

Couple number four is Bossy and Eric.
Couple number five is Secret and Keith.
Couple number six is Amber and Terry.
Couple number seven is Autumn and Tim.
Couple number eight is Derrick and Tonya.
Couple number nine is Christina and Aaron.

The last couple is Mason and me.

Game number two was called Eat the Banana. The men were told to hold a banana in front of their penis while the ladies had to peel the banana using their mouth only.

Game number three was a blindfolded game where one blindfold person had to sit in a chair with their hands tied. While blindfolded, a song of their choice was playing, and hands of the opposite sex were groping on them. The blindfolded person's job was to correctly guess who was touching on their body parts.

Game number four was a fun and active partner game. Couples had to pop a balloon while grinding on each other to the music, and the first couple to pop the balloon wins.

* * *

There were so many laughs between everyone, and it was a drama-free night. I'm sure there were long-lasting memories created between friends. We ended the night by playing spades and watching a movie.

CHAPTER 18

Christmas Time/ New Year's Eve and the End to the Beginning

"Good morning, Summer. It's time to wake up. It's Christmas…time to open up your presents!" Mason bellowed to wake me up.

We exchanged gifts at the same time. Mason's first gift was a Rolex watch, and my first gift was a Gucci pocketbook. Overall, I received a spa reservation, diamond bracelet and diamond earrings, red bottoms, clothes, and a custom-made dress for dinner. I brought Mason a new pair of boots, a leather jacket, Jordan's, and cologne.

Later in the afternoon, I stopped by Clark's house to drop off his gifts. His family was over visiting, and it was nice seeing his mother and father. Later in the evening, I made plans to stop by my parents' home for dinner and gift exchanging, where I will also see Autumn.

* * *

After a long week of being off, Autumn and I signed up for overtime before New Year's Eve. We will fly into Atlanta, and we return the next day back to Philadelphia. During my visit to Atlanta, I will see Mr. Biggam, and I'm more than so excited. Once Autumn and I arrived in

Atlanta, he picked us from the airport, and we agreed to stay at his place. Biggam and I were happy to see each other again, and he mentioned that he would like for me to meet his son since he's home from college because of the holiday.

* * *

Once we arrived at Biggam's place, I headed straight to the shower and changed for dinner. After my shower, Biggam handed me a red velvet long jewelry box, and inside was a blue sapphire necklace. I was excited to give him his gift and to see his reaction. I purchased him a Gucci men's Swiss Interlocking black leather strap watch. We kissed and hugged each other for a moment before we got dressed for our night out. He wore his new watch for the evening, and I was so happy to see that.

We headed to downtown Atlanta, enjoyed dinner at a fancy restaurant, and walked around. The weather and scenery were so perfect, and I enjoyed every moment.

* * *

On the flight back home, I was relaxed after the great evening Biggam, and I shared. I sat next to my sister, and we shared details about our quick trip to Atlanta.

"Autumn, you were passed out when I got in," I said to her.

"Well, Summer, I had some unexpected fun myself," she said with her sneaky smile.

I'm listening. I know you didn't have someone come to that man's house," I replied while cutting my eye at her.

"Hell no, sis, but his son came home and scared me," she said.

"Really, I met him this morning. He seems like a nice young man," I said to her.

"He's nice alright." She laughed.

"Autumn, what did you do?" I asked.

"Well, we started smoking, talking, laughing, and drinking. The next thing you know, we fucked, and I handcuffed him. He's a freak. He's only seven years younger than me, but he fucks good too," she said while smiling.

"Really? I'm completely shocked. He looks so innocent. You probably turned his ass out," I said to Autumn while laughing and shaking my head.

* * *

When I arrived back home, I had to get ready to pack for my New Year's Eve night in New York City. Mason and I planned to meet Angela so we can enjoy the last night of the year together. Traffic was crazy, and I know the city streets would be packed and filled with people. I know we are barely going to be able to move around once we got there.

When we finally met up with Angela, I was so happy to see her and to be able to get a massage with her. After all the working, traveling, and partying. My body could really use a nice rub down.

"Summer, baby, how are you doing?" Angela asked while hugging me.

"I'm okay, I just missed you like crazy. I've been working and sleeping a lot. Mason has been working so hard...all three of us need this day to ourselves," I explained to her.

Once we checked in at the hotel, we ordered room servers and stuffed our faces. The suite was huge, and from our level, we could look outside and see all the chaos. It was groups of people already holding their spots in front of the stage.

The masseuse knocked on the door around noon, and we were ready to get our full body massage and hot stone treatment. I was in complete peace, and the massage was so good it nearly put me to sleep.

"Mason, let's have a small session, lay up, and find a good movie to watch before dinner," I suggested.

It was now time for the three of us to go out to dinner, and Angela and I looked so sexy together. I wore a cut-out, body icon, sequin dress.

Angela wore a red split, one-sleeved dress, and Mason topped it off by wearing his Versace suit. Angela and I held on to each arm, and the three of us left for a lovely intimate dinner.

* * *

It was now after dinner, and we arrived back at the hotel suite. I rushed to the bathroom and began to barf in the toilet. Angela came in to help me and offered help. I told her that I really haven't been feeling too well lately.

"I really don't know. I haven't been feeling like myself lately," I sadly expressed to Angela.

"I have something to show you, Summer. I'll be right back," Angela quietly said.

She came back into the bathroom right away with a small store bag in her hand and pulled out a pregnancy test.

"Okay, so is that test positive or negative?" I asked.

"Well, I've been trying to tell you all day that I'm pregnant, and that's why I wasn't drinking," Angela said.

"Oh my god, wait, WHAT?" I asked loudly. I was utterly shocked. The news was so unexpected.

"Well...Summer, I think you should take a test also," Angela suggested.

Angela went down to the convenience store to get a pregnancy test and came back up to the room shortly after. She urged me to take the test, and I agreed. We patiently sat in the bathroom together after I peed on the stick, waiting for the results. We both looked at the test and saw two dark pink lines. Tears started running down my face. I was at a loss for words because I couldn't believe what I was hearing.

Mason knocked on the door to check on us and let us both know that the ball was about to drop. 20 down 10. 9. 8. 7. 6. 5. 4. 3. 2. 1! HAPPY NEW YEAR!!! We all hugged and kissed. Angela and I got to the balcony in our robes and slippers and screamed out Happy New Year to the crowd, and then we looked to each other and said out loud, "Well, who the fuck are the fathers?!"

Polyamory

"Polyamory emphasizes consciously choosing how many partners one wishes to be involved with rather than accepting social norms which dictate loving only one person at a time."

To be polyamorous means having open, intimate, or romantic relationships with more than one person at a time. People who are polyamorous can be heterosexual, lesbian, gay, or bisexual, and relationships between polyamorous people can include combinations of people of different sexual orientations.

Triad

Also known as a "throuple," a triad refers to a relationship with three people. Not all three people need to date one another. However, one person may be dating two different people.

Quad

As the name implies, a quad refers to a relationship with four people. This polyamorous relationship often occurs when two polyamorous couples meet and begin dating one person from the other couple. You can also have a full quad, where all four members are romantically or sexually involved with one another.

Polycule

This term refers to an entire network of people who are romantically connected. For example, it might include you and your primary partner, your primary partner's secondary partner, your primary partner's secondary partner's primary partner, and so on.

Kitchen Table Polyamory

This term refers to a family-like network formed by people who know each other. The name comes from the fact that people in this type of polyamorous relationship gather around the kitchen table for meals.

Parallel Polyamory

Parallel polyamory refers to relationships in which you're aware of each other's other partners but have little no contact with those partners.

Solo Polyamory

Individuals in a solo polyamorous relationship do not intend to merge their identity or life infrastructure with their partners. For example, they don't wish to marry or share a home or finances with any of their partners.
https://www.verywellmind.com/what-does-polyamorous-mean-21882

Po·lyg·a·my

/pəˈligəmē/
noun

1. the practice or custom of having more than one wife or husband at the same time.

Pol·y·an·dry

/ˈpälēˌandrē, ˌpäleˈandrē/
noun

1. polygamy in which a woman has more than one husband.

Pol·y·sex·u·al

/ˌpälē'sekSHo͞oəl/
adjective

    1.   incorporating many different kinds of sexuality; pansexual.

Mo·nog·a·my

/mə'nägəmē/
noun

    1.   the practice or state of being married to one person at a time.

O·pen Mar·riage

noun

Open Relationship

    1.   a marriage or relationship in which both partners agree that each may have sexual relations with others.

BDSM is a variety of often <u>erotic</u> practices or <u>roleplaying</u> involving <u>bondage</u>, <u>discipline</u>, <u>dominance and submission</u>, <u>sadomasochism</u>, and other related interpersonal dynamics. Given the wide range of practices, some of which may be engaged in by people who do not consider themselves to be practicing BDSM, inclusion in the BDSM community or subculture often is said to depend on <u>self-identification</u> and shared experience.

Swing·er

/ˈswiNGər/
noun

plural noun: **swingers**

1. INFORMAL
2. a lively and fashionable person who goes to a lot of social events. "One of the oldest swingers in town"
3. INFORMAL
4. a person who engages in group sex or the swapping of sexual partners.

What does *Erotic Cupping* mean?

Erotic cupping refers to a form of sensation play in which cups, bowls, or bells are used to create suction on the skin. Cupping is an ancient form of Chinese medicine, and it serves to bring blood to the skin and create intense sensations of localized pressure. The pressure, in itself, can be an erotic sensation, but drawing blood into the skin also makes it much more sensitive to other types of stimulation once the cups are removed.